SERVISTRY

THE MASTERY OF LEADERSHIP

DEEPAK SHARMA

Contents

Contents

Foreword

"True mastery lies not in authority, but in the courage to serve. In Servistry, leadership is a gift returned, not a title earned."

- Deepak Sharma

Preface

When I first set out to write Servistry, I wasn't just seeking to add another leadership book to the shelves. I wanted to offer something more — a perspective that challenges the conventional understanding of leadership itself. This book is a reflection of my personal journey, shaped by experiences, lessons, and the undeniable realization that leadership, at its core, is not about authority. It is about service.

Servistry is not a concept that emerged from a single moment of insight. It is the result of years spent observing, leading, and learning. I've seen organizations thrive when leaders prioritize people over power, and I've witnessed the ripple effect of leaders who choose to serve. These experiences led me to believe that service is not a compromise — it is a strength. It is the path to genuine leadership mastery.

Throughout this book, I invite you to explore what it means to lead with a service-first mindset. The chapters are not prescriptive manuals but reflections of real-world scenarios, thoughtful introspection, and the undeniable truth that leadership is a responsibility, not a privilege. You'll find stories, insights, and actionable approaches to embrace Servistry — whether you're leading a team, managing a business, or simply influencing those around you.

My hope is that Servistry sparks a shift in how you view leadership. I encourage you to engage deeply, question your current beliefs, and explore how these principles can shape your leadership style. Leadership is not a destination. It's an ongoing journey — one where each step you take in service of others strengthens your own growth and impact.

Thank you for choosing to be part of this journey. May your leadership story be one of service, courage, and lasting influence.

With gratitude and purpose,

Deepak Sharma

Acknowledgements

Writing Servistry has been a journey of reflection, learning, and growth. While this book carries my thoughts and experiences, it would not have been possible without the invaluable contributions of many individuals who have shaped my understanding of leadership.

First and foremost, I extend my deepest gratitude to the mentors and leaders who have guided me throughout my career. Their wisdom, encouragement, and sometimes even the tough lessons have been instrumental in shaping my perspective on leadership through service.

To my colleagues and teams — thank you for trusting my leadership and for challenging me to grow. Every experience we shared has enriched my understanding of what it means to lead with purpose and empathy. You have been my greatest teacher.

To my friends and family, your unwavering support and belief in me have been my anchor. Your patience and encouragement gave me the strength to turn my thoughts into words. I am forever grateful for your presence in my life.

A special note of thanks to the readers of Servistry. You are the heart of this movement. By choosing to engage with these ideas and explore the path of service-led leadership, you are contributing to a future where leadership is defined by impact, not authority.

Lastly, to every individual who serves — whether in a leadership role or through the simple act of making a difference — this book is dedicated to you. Your commitment to leading with purpose is the very essence of Servistry.

ACKNOWLEDGEMENTS

Thank you all for being part of this journey. May we continue to lead, serve, and grow together.

With immense gratitude,

Deepak Sharma

Synopsis

Servistry

The Mastery of Leadership

Through Service is a reimagining of leadership — one that shifts from authority to influence, from control to care. Through deep personal insights and practical reflections, this book invites readers to explore the power of leading with a service-first mindset.

Blending Service and Mastery, Servistry challenges conventional leadership norms. It speaks to leaders at all levels, from entrepreneurs to executives, encouraging them to unlock their full potential by putting people at the center of their leadership journey.

This isn't just a leadership model; it's a way of life. One that fosters cultures of trust, inspires innovation, and leaves a legacy of growth and empowerment.

The question isn't whether you have the authority to lead — it's whether you have the courage to serve.

Disclaimer

Servistry is a work of thought leadership based on the author's experiences, observations, and perspectives on service-led leadership. While every effort has been made to ensure the accuracy and applicability of the concepts discussed, the insights presented are intended for informational and reflective purposes only.

The scenarios, examples, and reflections within this book may draw from real-world leadership experiences; however, any resemblance to specific individuals, companies, or organizations is purely coincidental unless explicitly stated. Readers are encouraged to adapt the principles of Servistry to their unique circumstances, keeping in mind that outcomes may vary.

This book does not constitute professional, legal, financial, or psychological advice. The author and publisher disclaim any liability for decisions or actions taken based on the content of this book. Readers should seek appropriate professional guidance when making leadership or organizational decisions.

Additionally, Servistry promotes ethical leadership practices and respectful workplace environments. The application of these principles requires careful consideration of organizational culture, policies, and individual contexts.

Phase – I

The Foundation of Servistry

CHAPTER ONE

WHY SERVISTRY?

I still remember the moment I first questioned the way leadership is traditionally taught. It wasn't in a classroom or a seminar. It was in the middle of a high-stakes business decision, where the weight of authority and responsibility clashed with the reality of people.

I had seen leadership in many forms—some driven by control, others by charisma. But something always felt missing. The most effective leaders I had worked with weren't the loudest in the room, nor the ones who demanded the most. They were the ones who created impact through service—leaders who mastered not just the art of leadership, but the art of enabling others to thrive.

That realization led me to Servistry—a belief that leadership is not about status or authority, but about mastery in serving others to create extraordinary results. It's a word that blends "Service" and "Mastery" because leadership is an ongoing craft. You don't just serve. You become exceptional at it.

This book is not about theories. It's about a fundamental shift in leadership—a shift I've experienced firsthand, one that changed the way I lead and the way I see leadership shaping the future of business.

Leadership as We Knew It

For decades, leadership has been defined by hierarchy. The assumption was that authority meant influence, and control meant effectiveness. But times have changed. Organizations are realizing that positional power no longer guarantees commitment.

I've seen up close — leaders with impressive titles struggling to inspire their teams. Strategies well-documented on paper but failing in execution because people weren't truly engaged. It was never a lack of knowledge, but a lack of connection.

That's when I knew: The future of leadership isn't about leading from the top down. It's about leading from within.

I started observing the leaders who thrived, the ones people followed not because they had to, but because they wanted to. And the pattern became clear—they all led through service.

They empowered instead of dictated.

They created trust instead of fear.

They built organizations where people weren't just employees, they were invested contributors.

This wasn't about making leadership "softer." It was about making it stronger, more human, and more effective.

How Servistry Was Born

Servistry wasn't just a concept I read about. It was something I lived and tested—through tough leadership moments, business challenges, and personal experiences.

I had to unlearn parts of leadership I once thought was essential. I had to let go of the idea that power and control were the ultimate tools of influence. Instead, I learned that real influence comes from service, trust, and the ability to bring out the best in others.

I also saw the data. The most successful organizations, whether startups or Fortune 500 companies, had one thing in common: leaders who understood that their role was to serve, not just to lead.

- **Satya Nadella** transformed Microsoft not through authority, but through empathy and trust.
- **Howard Schultz** built Starbucks into a global brand by prioritizing employees and creating a culture of shared ownership.
- **Indra Nooyi** made PepsiCo thrive not just with business acumen, but by putting people at the center.

These were not accidental successes. They were the result of leaders practicing Servistry, whether they called it that or not.

Servistry: A New Leadership Standard

This book isn't just about discussing leadership, it's about challenging it. I'm not here to say traditional leadership doesn't work. I'm here to say there's a better way.

Servistry isn't about abandoning authority. It's about using it differently—not as a tool for control, but as a responsibility to serve.

It's about shifting from:

- Leading through hierarchy → Leading through trust
- Commanding action → Creating ownership

- Being the smartest in the room → Enabling the best ideas to surface

This isn't a leadership "trend." It's a necessity. The organizations that embrace this shift will win in the long run. Those that resist will struggle with disengagement, low retention, and a workforce that simply doesn't care.

Servistry is the difference between leaders who demand results and leaders who inspire them

Why This Book? Why Now?

I didn't write this book to add another leadership framework to the pile. I wrote it because I believe this shift is urgent.

I've seen what happens when leaders cling to outdated authority models; they fight resistance at every step. I've also seen what happens when leaders embrace Servistry—their teams perform better, their influence grows naturally, and their impact lasts beyond their tenure.

This book is my way of making sure leaders don't just keep up with change but lead it.

In the coming chapters, I'll take you deeper into the psychology, the real-world applications, and the step-by-step transformation that turns Servistry from an idea into a leadership standard.

Because leadership isn't about power. It's about impact. And impact is built through service.

CHAPTER TWO

THE PSYCHOLOGY OF SERVICE

I've always been fascinated by what truly drives people. Not just in business, but in life. *Why do some people give their best effort, while others do the bare minimum? Why do some teams thrive under leadership, while others resist or disengage?*

For a long time, leadership was framed as a question of authority—who had the power, who made the decisions, who were expected to follow. But the more I observed, the clearer it became people who don't follow authority. They follow belief.

Belief in a purpose.
Belief in a leader's intent.
Belief that their contributions matter.

That's where service comes in—not as an abstract leadership philosophy, but as a deeply rooted psychological driver that determines how people respond to leadership itself.

What Science Tells Us About Leadership and Service

There's an undeniable link between service and influence. Neuroscience and behavioral studies have proven that humans are wired to reciprocate positive leadership behaviors. When people feel valued, trusted, and empowered, their brain releases oxytocin—the "bonding" hormone that strengthens trust and collaboration.

Think about the leaders who have made the biggest impact in your life. They probably weren't the ones who commanded authority. They were the ones who created trust.

The truth is people don't resist leadership itself. They resist feeling like they don't matter.

Studies in organizational psychology show that employees who feel genuinely supported by their leaders are 87% more engaged and 40% more likely to stay with a company long-term. Not because they are paid more. Not because they are forced to. But because they feel valued.

So why do so many leaders still struggle with engagement, motivation, and retention?
Because they misunderstand power.

The Leadership Power Shift

Traditional leadership models have conditioned us to think of power as something leaders hold over others. The stronger the control, the more effective the leadership. But the real psychology of leadership tells a different story.

People are most engaged not when they are controlled, but when they are empowered.

The best leaders don't lead from the top. They create environments where people feel safe to take initiative, contribute, and grow. That's what real influence looks like.

I remember a conversation with a senior executive—let's call him Ramesh. He was struggling with his team. Performance was dipping, morale was low, and despite increasing targets and tightening controls, results weren't improving.

"What's the issue?" I asked him.

"They don't seem motivated," he said. "They have everything—good pay, benefits, job security. I don't understand why they aren't putting in more effort."

I asked him a simple question: "Do they feel like their work matters?"

He paused. He had never considered that before.

Over the next few months, he changed his approach. Instead of just setting targets, he spent time understanding his team's goals and concerns. He started recognizing their contributions in meaningful ways. He involved them in decisions rather than just passing down directives.

The result? His team's performance skyrocketed. Not because of new policies, but because they finally felt valued.

That's the shift from authority to service. It's a psychological unlock that turns compliance into commitment.

Why Service is the Strongest Leadership Strategy

Many leaders resist the idea of service because they think it makes leadership weaker—as if serving others means giving up control. The reality is the opposite.

Servant leaders are more powerful because their influence isn't dependent on fear, pressure, or compliance. It's built on trust, inspiration, and human connection.

The world's best leaders understand this intuitively.

- **Satya Nadella** didn't turn Microsoft around by demanding better results. He did it by reshaping the culture, encouraging learning, embracing empathy, and making leadership about enabling rather than commanding.
- **Howard Schultz** built Starbucks into a global powerhouse not just by selling coffee, but by creating an organization where employees felt invested and cared for.
- **Indra Nooyi** transformed PepsiCo with the philosophy that leadership is about serving a higher purpose—whether it's employees, customers, or society.

The common thread? *They didn't just manage companies. They created cultures where people wanted to excel.*

The Service Mindset: A Personal Shift

For years, I believed leadership was about having the right answers, making big decisions, setting the direction. And to some extent, that's true. But the biggest shift in my own leadership journey came when I realized that my job wasn't just to lead.

It was to serve.
To create environments where people feel psychologically safe.
To make sure they felt their work had meaning.
To inspire them to be their best—not because they had to, but because they wanted to.
That's what Servistry is about. It's not just a leadership style—it's a leadership advantage.

In the next chapter, we'll go even deeper. If leadership isn't about authority, then where does power really come from? And how do we shift our influence in a way that makes people want to follow, rather than feel forced to?

Let's explore that next.

CHAPTER THREE

Beyond Authority – The Power Shift

I've often wondered: *Why do we listen to some leaders effortlessly, while resisting others, even if they hold authority?*

For years, leadership was synonymous with control. The assumption was simple—if you hold the title, the position, the power, people will follow. But time and again, reality has proven otherwise.

I've seen CEOs who struggled to influence their own teams. Managers whose teams disengaged despite their expertise. Leaders who, despite having every tool of authority, found themselves fighting for real influence.

And I've also seen leaders—some without formal authority—who commanded deep loyalty, inspired action, and built cultures where people went beyond expectations.

The difference? *True leadership power doesn't come from authority. It comes from something much deeper.*

This is the power shift that Servistry embraces—a shift from leading through position to leading through purpose.

The Illusion of Authority

We often assume that leadership is about being in charge. After all, titles and hierarchies exist for a reason. But here's the hard truth:

Authority can force compliance, but it cannot create commitment.

People might follow instructions because they have to, but they'll only give their best when they want to.

I once worked with a senior leader—let's call him Vikram—who had all the hallmarks of authority. A top executive in a global firm, highly accomplished, respected on paper. But despite his credentials, his team struggled.

Projects stalled. Innovation was slow. Morale was low.

He couldn't understand it. "I've built this team; I've given them direction. Why do I still have to push for results?"

The issue wasn't strategy. It wasn't intelligence. It was the fact that his leadership relied on authority but lacked connection.

People saw him as a boss, not a leader.

I remember sitting down with him and asking:

"How many people on your team would voluntarily follow you if they weren't required to?" The silence that followed said everything.

Where Real Power Comes From

If authority alone isn't enough, then what makes people follow?
It's not fear.
It's not control.
It's not even financial incentives.
It's something far more human—a combination of trust, inspiration, and shared purpose.

Research from Harvard Business Review shows that employees who trust their leaders are 76% more engaged and 50% more productive than those who feel disconnected.

And trust isn't built through policies or processes. It's built through leadership that serves, supports, and elevates people.

That's why the most effective leaders don't rely on their position. They build influence in three key takeaways':

- **Authenticity** – People follow leaders who are real, not just authoritative.
- **Empathy** – Leaders who understand and care about their teams create deeper commitment.
- **Service** – When people see that leadership isn't about personal gain, but about enabling others, they reciprocate with loyalty.

This is the real power shift.

Breaking Free from Traditional Leadership

The leaders who thrive today are those who recognize that the workplace has changed. People don't work just for salaries—they work for meaning.

Traditional leadership says: *"I am in charge, so you must follow."*

Servistry says: *"I serve a purpose, and people follow because they believe in it."*

We've seen this shift across the world:

- **Elon Musk** doesn't lead Tesla with traditional authority—his employees are driven by a vision of innovation.
- **Jacinda Ardern** reshaped political leadership with empathy and connection rather than force.
- **Tony Hsieh** built Zappos into a culture where people thrived, not because of corporate rules, but because they felt ownership.

None of these leaders relied purely on position. They led through impact.

And that's what today's workforce demands—leaders who don't just instruct but inspire.

Servistry in Action: A Personal Shift

I didn't always understand this shift. Early in my leadership journey, I believed influence came from knowing the most, deciding the fastest, and making the toughest calls.

I thought leadership meant standing at the top, directing the way.

But as I grew, I realized that my greatest leadership moments weren't when I had the answers. They were when I empowered others to find them.

The first time I let go of control and allowed my team to take ownership, I expected chaos. Instead, I saw engagement, creativity, and results beyond what I could have achieved alone.

That's when I knew: Real leadership is not about being at the top. It's about building people up.

The Future of Leadership: The Power Shift Begins

Organizations that cling to authority-driven leadership will struggle. The future belongs to leaders who understand this power shift.

A shift from control to collaboration.
From authority to authenticity.
From being in charge to being in service.
This isn't a soft leadership philosophy—it's the most effective way to lead in the modern world.

And as we move forward in this journey, one question remains: *How do we put Servistry into action in real business environments?*

That's exactly what we'll explore next.

CHAPTER FOUR

SERVICE VS. SERVISTRY

For years, I believed that service was the highest form of leadership. It felt right—being available for others, putting their needs first, ensuring that they felt supported and valued.

And yet, I couldn't shake an unsettling reality.

Some of the most service-oriented leaders I knew—those who poured their energy into their teams—often struggled to create lasting impact. Their efforts were appreciated, even admired, but something was missing.

I saw managers who were constantly giving, yet their teams remained stagnant.
I saw leaders who made themselves accessible, yet decisions still fell solely on them.
I saw cultures that emphasized support yet lacked momentum.

It didn't make sense. If service was the answer, why wasn't it enough?

It took me years to recognize the missing piece. Service alone doesn't automatically lead to leadership. True leadership demands something more—a level of mastery, intention, and impact that goes beyond service.

And that's what led me to Servistry.

The Subtle but Powerful Difference

To the outside world, service and Servistry may seem similar. After all, both involve helping others, prioritizing people, and leading with care.

But the difference is profound.
Service is about supporting people.
Servistry is about elevating people.

Service can be passive—it's the act of assisting, responding, and being available. But Servistry is active—it's intentional leadership that blends service with expertise, vision, and execution.

I learned this lesson the hard way.

A Leadership Misstep That Changed My Perspective

Early in my leadership journey, I had a team that I cared deeply about. I made it my mission to ensure they felt heard, valued, and empowered. I was there for them, day in and day out.

I thought I was doing everything right. And for a while, it worked. Morale was high. Engagement was strong. People trusted me. But then something unexpected happened.

A major business challenge arose, and when I looked to my team to take ownership, they hesitated. They looked back at me—not for guidance, but for direction.

That's when it hit me. I had built trust, but not capability. I had supported them, but I hadn't stretched them. I had created comfort, but I hadn't pushed them toward growth.

It wasn't their fault. It was mine.

I had been serving them—but I had not been leading them to mastery.
That was the day I understood the gap between service and Servistry.

Where Leaders Get Stuck

I've seen this pattern repeat itself in organizations worldwide.

- *Leaders who are too focused on service often struggle to drive accountability and growth.*
- *Leaders who are too focused on authority often struggle to build trust and loyalty.*

The sweet spot lies in Servistry—where service is not just about kindness but about creating transformation.

Servistry isn't just about helping people do their jobs—it's about helping them become leaders themselves.

And that requires something far beyond service—it requires a commitment to both support and challenge, both care and capability, both empathy and expectation.

The Mindset Shift: Moving from Service to Servistry

Think about it like this.

A service-oriented leader asks: *"How can I make things easier for my team?"*

A Servistry-driven leader asks: *"How can I make my team stronger?"*

One builds dependence. The other builds growth.
One creates comfort. The other creates capability.
One earns appreciation. The other earns legacy.

And the world needs more leaders who are ready to lead with Servistry—leaders who don't just serve but elevate those around them to their highest potential.

The Question That Every Leader Must Ask

As I reflect on my own leadership journey, one question has stayed with me:
Am I leading in a way that makes my team stronger even when I'm not around?

Because that's the true test. Leadership is not about how much people need you. It's about how much they grow because of you.

And that is the essence of Servistry.

In the next chapter, we'll go deeper— what does it truly mean to develop leaders instead of followers?
That's the next evolution of this journey

CHAPTER FIVE

EMPATHY AS A LEADERSHIP SKILL

I still remember the silence that filled the room.

It was a leadership meeting, the kind where the air was usually charged with energy — ideas flying, numbers flashing on screens, and voices layered in discussion. But this time, it was different.

The numbers weren't in our favour. The pressure was palpable. And then, a senior leader made a remark — sharp, calculated, decisive. It was the kind of comment that usually sealed the direction of a conversation. Yet, something about it didn't sit right with me.

I glanced around the room. Some nodded, others hesitated. But the real story wasn't in their words — it was in their eyes. Uncertainty lingered; questions remained unspoken. It would have been easy to move on, to follow the path laid before us.

But instead, I chose to pause.
Not to argue, not to challenge, but to ask a simple question:

"What's on your mind?"

It was a moment of choice — one that had nothing to do with

authority or intellect. It had everything to do with **empathy**.

The Misunderstood Power of Empathy

Empathy is often reduced to the ability to understand others' feelings — a polite nod to emotional awareness. But in the world of leadership, empathy is far more than that.

It's not just about feeling — it's about perceiving. Not just about understanding — but about acting on that understanding. Empathy is what allows leaders to sense the unspoken, read between the lines, and step into perspectives that are not their own.

But it wasn't always my strongest suit.

When I Missed the Signs

Earlier in my career, I prided myself on decisiveness. I believed leaders were expected to have clear answers — to navigate uncertainty with unwavering confidence. And in my attempt to lead with certainty, I often missed the undercurrents of emotion that shaped the room.

I recall a project where deadlines were slipping. My instincts told me to fix the problem with sharper deadlines, clearer expectations, and more frequent check-ins. On paper, it seemed like leadership. But beneath the surface, frustration was festering.

What I didn't see then was the emotional toll — the burnout, the fear of failure, the unspoken pressure. I had managed the task, but I had failed the people.

It took one honest conversation — a brave employee telling me how overwhelmed the team felt — for me to realize the blind spot I carried. Decisions without empathy are like blueprints without foundations — they may look solid, but they crumble under pressure.

The Shift to Empathetic Leadership

Empathy in leadership didn't mean losing my decisiveness. It meant sharpening it.

When I started leading with empathy, conversations changed. People felt seen. They brought their challenges forward, not because they feared consequences, but because they trusted I would listen.

And when people trust you with their truth, you gain something no strategy can replace — clarity.

Empathy became my compass. It didn't mean avoiding tough decisions. It meant making them with a complete understanding — of the people they impacted and the emotions they carried.

The Three Layers of Empathy

As I deepened my practice of empathetic leadership, I came to see it as more than a single trait. It was layered, nuanced, and ever evolving.

- *Self-awareness*: *Understanding my own biases and emotional responses.*
- *Active Listening*: *Not just hearing words but observing what remains unspoken.*
- *Courageous Action*: *Responding in ways that uplift others, even when it's uncomfortable.*

Every leader will face moments where empathy is tested. Moments where it feels easier to lead from authority than from understanding. But it's in those very moments that the choice to lead with empathy defines us.

A Moment That Redefined My Leadership

There was a day when a colleague walked into my office — visibly anxious. They spoke of a mistake that had impacted a major client. It would have been easy to respond with frustration, to question their competence.

But something held me back.

I chose to listen. Not just to the details of the mistake, but to the fear woven into their words. They weren't just afraid of the consequences — they were afraid of losing trust.

That day, I didn't respond with reprimand. I responded with partnership. We worked through the solution together. And from that moment, their confidence soared. Not because the mistake was forgotten, but because they knew they were valued beyond their failures.

That's empathy in leadership — the ability to turn moments of fear into moments of growth.

Reflections for Every Leader

Empathy is not a finite resource. The more we practice it, the more it expands. And as leaders, it's our responsibility to cultivate it — not just for ourselves, but within our teams.

So, I leave you with a question that I continue to ask myself:

"Am I leading in a way that invites truth, or am I leading in a way that silences it?"

Because the greatest leaders are not those who know all the answers. They are those who create spaces where answers can emerge — from the minds, hearts, and voices of others.

And in that space, Servistry thrives.

LEADING WITH PURPOSE

I've often wondered — what truly separates a leader from a manager? Both may excel at execution, drive performance, and ensure results. But a leader, a true leader, carries something far less tangible yet infinitely more powerful.

Purpose

Purpose is not simply about hitting targets or climbing corporate ladders. It's not found in mission statements plastered on office walls. Purpose lives in the quiet decisions we make, the causes we champion, and the people we choose to serve.

I didn't fully understand this until I found myself at a crossroads.

When Purpose Became Personal

There was a time when my career trajectory was clear — or so I thought. I was leading with confidence, delivering results, and gaining recognition. From the outside, it seemed like success. But on the inside, something was missing.

I remember sitting in yet another meeting, discussing quarterly projections and market positioning. Every decision was logical, well-informed, and precise. Yet, I walked away feeling hollow. The work was important, no doubt, but I couldn't shake the question that lingered:

"Why does this matter?"

It wasn't about rejecting ambition or questioning the need for results. It was about discovering whether those results were contributing to something larger than myself.

That moment marked the beginning of my search for purpose.

Purpose Is Not a Grand Revelation

Many believe purpose arrives like a lightning bolt — a sudden realization that changes everything. But in my experience, it's rarely that dramatic.

Purpose often reveals itself quietly. It unfolds in the seemingly ordinary moments — a challenging conversation with a colleague, a decision to support an employee's growth, or the choice to stand by a value when it's inconvenient.

Looking back, I see that purpose had always been present. It was there when I mentored a struggling teammate instead of focusing solely on my own goals. It was there when I stayed late to help a colleague meet a deadline, not because I had to, but because I wanted to.

Service, I realized, was not a separate act. It was the very essence of my purpose. And through Servistry, purpose became my compass.

The Difference Between Serving and Pleasing

There's a misconception that leading with purpose means endlessly pleasing others. But service-led leadership is not about sacrificing your values or bending to every demand.

Purpose is about discerning where your service is most meaningful. It's about knowing when to stand firm and when to adapt. It's recognizing that true service sometimes means making hard decisions — not to protect your image, but to protect the mission.

I recall a moment when I had to challenge the status quo. A decision was on the table that would have driven immediate financial gain but at the cost of long-term employee well-being. The numbers said "yes," but my purpose said otherwise.

Speaking up wasn't easy. It never is. But when you lead with purpose, the discomfort of the moment is outweighed by the clarity of your conviction.

And that clarity? It inspires others to do the same.

Purpose Is a Collective Force

One of the greatest lessons I've learned is that purpose is rarely a solo pursuit. While it may begin as a personal revelation, its true power emerges when it's shared.

I've seen teams transform when they align around a common purpose. Meetings shift from transactional to meaningful. Difficult conversations become opportunities for growth. People stop asking, "What's in it for me?" and start asking, "How can we make a difference?"

But this alignment doesn't happen by accident. Leaders must actively cultivate it.

- *Invite Conversations About Purpose: Ask your team why their work matters to them. You may be surprised by the depth of their answers.*
- *Connect Tasks to Impact: Every spreadsheet, presentation, and project contributes to something larger. Make that connection visible.*
- *Recognize Purpose in Action: Celebrate moments when people choose the mission over personal comfort. Those are the stories that build culture.*

When people see that their service has meaning, they don't just work harder — they work with heart. And no incentive can replicate that.

The Courage to Course Correct

Purpose is not static. It evolves as we grow, as our experiences shape us, and as the world around us changes.

There was a time when I clung to goals that no longer served my mission. I had convinced myself that persistence was a sign of strength. But in truth, strength sometimes lies in the courage to pause, reflect, and realign.

Walking away from something that no longer aligns with your purpose is not failure. It's integrity.

And it's in those moments — when you choose purpose over pride — that you lead not just with your mind, but with your soul.

A Personal Reflection

If I were to distil everything I've learned about purpose into one question, it would be this:

"If no one was watching, would I still choose this path?"

Because purpose isn't about applause or external validation. It's about knowing that what you do — and how you do it — aligns with who you are.

That's the essence of Servistry. Not service for recognition, but service because it's right. Not leadership for authority, but leadership for impact.

And when you lead with purpose, the people around you won't just follow. They'll believe.

As you navigate your own leadership journey, consider these questions:

- *What moments have made you feel most aligned with your purpose?*
- *Are there areas where you're leading out of habit, rather than intention?*
- *How can you connect your daily actions to something greater?*

Because at the end of the day, titles fade. Profits rise and fall. But the impact you make — through purposeful service — leaves a legacy that endures.

And that legacy? That's the true mark of leadership.

Phase – II

Servistry in Action

CHAPTER SEVEN

BUILDING A SERVICE CULTURE

The real test of Servistry isn't in individual actions — it's in how deeply it is embedded into the organization. Many companies talk about a "customer-first" approach or a "people-centric" culture. But there's a significant difference between words on a wall and behaviours in a hallway.

I remember walking into an organization years ago — the lobby was filled with framed values like "Integrity," "Excellence," and "Customer Focus." The words were polished, but the atmosphere felt cold. Employees avoided eye contact, conversations were rushed, and collaboration seemed more like a formality than a choice.

It was clear that the values were aspirational — not actual.

On the other hand, I've witnessed companies where Servistry was alive in every interaction. You could see it in how managers supported their teams, how cross-functional collaboration thrived, and how customer feedback wasn't just collected — it was celebrated. The difference? Servistry wasn't a program. It was the organization's pulse.

In this chapter, we'll explore how to turn Servistry into more than a concept. We'll understand how leaders, systems, and everyday choices contribute to a service culture that endures.

Why Culture Eats Strategy for Breakfast

Peter Drucker famously said, "Culture eats strategy for breakfast." It's a reminder that no matter how well-defined a strategy is, it will crumble without the right cultural foundation.

Servistry is not a stand-alone initiative; it's an operating philosophy. When organizations build a culture of Servistry, it doesn't just impact customer satisfaction — it transforms how employees engage, innovate, and lead.

But what does that look like in practice?

I recall a mid-sized company I worked with, where attrition rates were climbing, and employee engagement was at an all-time low. Leaders were puzzled. On paper, they had done everything right — competitive salaries, rewards programs, even flexible work policies. Yet people were disengaged.

When we dug deeper, the issue wasn't a lack of benefits — it was a lack of belonging. Employees didn't feel seen or valued. Decisions were made from boardrooms without the perspective of those on the ground. Leadership felt distant.

That's when Servistry came into focus.

Embedding Servistry: A Leadership Responsibility

A service culture begins at the top. Leaders are the custodians of culture, and their behaviours send ripples across the organization.

One particular leader I admire, a CEO of a fast-growing tech firm, embodied Servistry without ever using the term. He spent the first hour of his week calling customers directly, not to solve problems, but to listen. He would often say, "The people we serve know what we should learn."

This act of listening cascaded down the organization. Managers began holding open forums with their teams, not to dictate, but to gather insights. The leadership team restructured performance reviews to include questions like:

Who have you served this quarter?
What impact did your service create?
How can we enable you to serve better?

It was no surprise that employee satisfaction skyrocketed — not because of grand incentives, but because people felt their voices mattered.

Systems that Sustain Servistry

While leadership ignites culture, systems sustain it. Servistry must be built into the very fabric of how decisions are made, how success is measured, and how people are rewarded.

Think about how most organizations measure performance. The focus often leans heavily on financial results. While those metrics are important, they rarely tell the full story. In a Servistry-led organization, metrics shift to include:

- *Customer Advocacy: Not just satisfaction scores, but genuine stories of how the company made a difference.*
- *Employee Well-Being: Measuring psychological safety, growth opportunities, and meaningful recognition.*

- *Service Impact: Evaluating how internal teams support one another, fostering collaboration and knowledge sharing.*

One company I worked with introduced a "Service Multiplier" metric. Departments weren't only evaluated on their direct results, but also on how they empowered others. Finance, for example, wasn't just assessed on budget adherence but on how effectively they enabled frontline teams.

This shift didn't just elevate collaboration — it dismantled silos. Servistry became the language of success.

Hiring for Servistry

Culture is built one hire at a time. If Servistry is the aspiration, it should be evident in who the organization brings onboard.

I recall a hospitality chain that made service a non-negotiable hiring criterion. During interviews, candidates weren't only assessed on their qualifications — they were asked to share stories of service. Not in grand gestures, but in everyday moments.

One candidate shared how, as a barista, they memorized the names and preferences of regular customers. It wasn't required; it was simply a choice to serve with intention. That small act of service said far more than any resume could.

Organizations committed to Servistry ask:

- *Does this person see leadership as an opportunity to serve?*
- *Do they listen to understand, not just to respond?*
- *Can they foster psychological safety for others?*

Skills can be trained. Mindsets are cultivated. Hiring for Servistry is an investment in both.

When Culture Becomes DNA

Perhaps the greatest marker of a successful service culture is when Servistry becomes instinctive. You no longer need posters or campaigns to remind people of the values — they live them.

I once asked an employee in a purpose-driven healthcare organization how they defined their culture. Without hesitation, they replied:

"We take care of each other so we can take care of others."

It wasn't a scripted response. It was how they operated. When a colleague was struggling, others stepped in. When a patient needed extra care, they found a way. And when mistakes happened, they focused on learning instead of blame.

That's Servistry — not as a statement, but as a shared belief.

As you think about your own organization, consider these questions:

- *Is service genuinely valued, or is it treated as a function of customer support?*
- *How often are people recognized for serving others — internally or externally?*
- *What systems reinforce or discourage acts of service?*
- *If a new employee joined today, how long would it take for them to experience Servistry firsthand?*

Building a service culture is not a one-time effort. It's a continuous commitment — a leadership choice that echoes through every interaction.

As service becomes embedded in the fabric of your organization, decision-making takes on a new form. Leaders no longer operate from a top-down perspective but from a place of service.

And when that choice becomes the norm, Servistry doesn't just shape the culture. It becomes the culture.

CHAPTER EIGHT

SERVANT DECISION-MAKING

How Service-Oriented Leaders Make Better Business Choices

Decision-making is often seen as the ultimate test of leadership. The weight of responsibility, the pressure of uncertainty, and the ever-present demand for results can turn even the simplest choices into complex dilemmas. But when leaders adopt the mindset of Servistry, the way they approach decisions fundamentally shifts.

Instead of asking, "What benefits me?" or even "What benefits the business?" they ask:

- *"Who are we serving?"*
- *"How will this decision impact those we serve?"*
- *"What is the most responsible and service-oriented choice we can make?"*

It's not a mindset of sacrifice or selflessness to the point of weakness. Rather, it's about recognizing that sustainable success is the product of decisions that prioritize long-term service over short-term gains.

A Decision That Changed My Perspective

I remember a particular moment early in my career when I was faced with a challenging decision. We had to restructure a key department due to declining performance. On paper, the numbers were clear — reducing the headcount would immediately ease operational costs. It seemed like the most "logical" choice.

But something about that logic felt incomplete.

I chose to pause. Instead of rushing to implement what the data suggested, I spent days talking to employees, managers, and even customers who were directly impacted by the department's work. What I uncovered was not a problem of inefficiency, but a problem of disconnection. Teams felt unheard, frontline employees were overwhelmed, and innovation had stalled.

The decision shifted. Instead of cutting the team, we chose to redesign workflows, redistribute responsibilities, and provide support where it was needed most. The result? Performance rebounded, engagement soared, and the organization retained experienced talent.

That moment taught me that the best decisions aren't always the fastest or the easiest. They're the ones made with service in mind.

The Three Dimensions of Servant Decision-Making

Leaders who embrace Servistry evaluate choices across three dimensions:

1. Impact on People:

Every decision affect people — employees, customers, partners, and communities. Leaders in Servistry consider these human impacts alongside financial metrics.

- Will this choice empower or disengage our people?
- Are we listening to those affected by the decision?
- How can we mitigate negative impacts and create positive ones?

2. Long-Term Value Creation:

Service-led leaders think beyond quarterly results. They ask:

- How will this decision serve the long-term purpose of the organization?
- Will it build trust or erode it?
- Are we solving a symptom or addressing the root cause?

3. Alignment with Purpose:

Servistry ensures decisions remain aligned with the organization's core mission.

- Does this choice align with our values?
- Will we be proud of this decision years from now?
- Are we holding ourselves accountable to our principles?

When Service-Led Decisions Defy Convention

Some of the most remarkable business decisions stem from leaders choosing service over short-term logic.

Consider the story of a well-known global airline that faced a surge of flight delays. While industry norms would suggest cutting operational corners to stay on schedule, their CEO took a different route. He empowered ground staff to delay flights when necessary, prioritizing safety and respectful service over punctuality.

The decision didn't just.prevent potential accidents — it enhanced customer loyalty. Passengers saw that the airline valued their safety more than their on-time rating. This seemingly "costly" decision ultimately built long-term trust and advocacy.

The lesson? When leaders decide with Servistry, they often trade immediate wins for enduring impact.

Decision-Making Under Pressure

Service-oriented decision-making is particularly tested in moments of crisis. During economic downturns or operational challenges, leaders may feel tempted to prioritize survival above service. But Servistry is not about choosing one over the other — it's about recognizing that true resilience comes from serving stakeholders well.

A leader I deeply respect once faced a supply chain crisis that threatened to delay product delivery for thousands of customers. While competitors cut corners to meet timelines, this leader chose transparency. They informed customers about the delay, provided regular updates, and offered proactive support.

The result? Instead of losing trust, the company strengthened its customer relationships. People valued the honesty and effort. That's the power of Servistry in moments of adversity.

Empowering Others to Decide with Servistry

Servant decision-making is not the responsibility of a single leader. It's a collective mindset that permeates the entire organization. The most effective leaders empower their teams to make service-led choices by:

1. Providing Context, Not Just Instructions:

When people understand the "why" behind a decision, they're more likely to make aligned choices on their own. Leaders should consistently communicate the broader mission and purpose.

2. Creating Psychological Safety:

Employees are more likely to make bold, service-oriented decisions when they know they won't be punished for mistakes. Establishing a culture of learning over blame is essential.

3. Recognizing and Celebrating Servistry in Action:

Acknowledge and reward decisions that prioritize service — not just those that generate immediate results. Stories of service-led choices should be amplified across the organization.

Pause and reflect on your own leadership decisions:

- *Can you recall a time when you prioritized service over short-term gains?*
- *How do you ensure your decisions align with the long-term well-being of people and the organization?*
- *Are there voices you may be overlooking in your decision-making process?*

Servant decision-making isn't about avoiding difficult choices. It's about making those choices with integrity, empathy, and a commitment to serve.

Because in the end, the legacy of a leader is not defined by the number of decisions they make — but by the lives they impact through those decisions.

Effective decision-making is only possible in an environment where people feel psychologically safe. Leaders who prioritize service cultivate trust, encouraging diverse perspectives and constructive dialogue. In the next chapter, we'll uncover how creating psychological safety strengthens both people and performance.

CHAPTER NINE

PSYCHOLOGICAL SAFETY AND TRUST

Trust is not declared; it is felt. It's the quiet confidence that you can speak up without fear, knowing your ideas and concerns will be respected. In the landscape of leadership, creating this sense of safety is not just admirable — it's essential. Psychological safety, a term popularised by organizational researcher Amy Edmondson, refers to the belief that one can take interpersonal risks without facing judgment or retaliation. But in the context of Servistry, it's something even deeper. It is the belief that leadership is fundamentally about service — and when leaders serve, they create spaces where trust thrives.

A Moment of Reflection

I remember a time early in my leadership journey when a junior colleague hesitated to voice a concern during a critical project. After several attempts to encourage openness, I realized the problem wasn't hesitation — it was fear. Fear of being seen as incompetent. Fear of retribution. And, perhaps most telling, fear of irrelevance.

That experience stayed with me. I questioned myself: Had I created a culture of compliance instead of courage? It was then I understood — trust is not built by simply inviting feedback. It is built when people believe their voice will lead to meaningful change.

Beyond the Surface of Trust

Many organizations claim to prioritize psychological safety. They conduct surveys, host town halls, and establish "open-door" policies. Yet, these gestures often remain symbolic if the underlying culture discourages dissent. Servistry calls for a more intentional approach. It's not about merely tolerating differences — it's about celebrating them.

A leader practicing Servistry does not wait for the absence of fear. Instead, they work to dissolve it. They understand that when people feel genuinely safe, they contribute more boldly, innovate freely, and challenge assumptions constructively. This isn't just about making employees "comfortable" — it's about empowering them to act in service of a greater purpose.

The Leader's Role in Building Trust

Leadership decisions, both big and small, set the tone for psychological safety. Consider how you respond to failure. Do you treat it as a learning moment, or does it become a source of shame? Do you recognize contributions openly, or are successes claimed by a select few? Servistry requires leaders to view these moments as opportunities to build resilience and trust.

There is immense power in a simple phrase like, "I don't have all the answers." Vulnerability signals confidence, not weakness. When leaders acknowledge their own limitations, they create space for others to step in with ideas and solutions. Trust flourishes in these gaps.

Trust as a Business Multiplier

The absence of trust has measurable costs — disengagement, turnover, and lost innovation. On the other hand, organizations with a strong culture of psychological safety consistently outperform their peers. Teams collaborate with greater agility, ideas are tested and improved faster, and leaders are more attuned to emerging risks.

In Servistry, the mindset shifts from "How can I lead better?" to "How can I serve better?" The result is a ripple effect — a workforce that feels empowered to contribute, challenge, and grow.

A Commitment to Safety

Building psychological safety is not a one-time initiative. It's an ongoing commitment. And it starts with you. Begin by listening with curiosity instead of judgment. Celebrate vulnerability. Model the courage to speak the truth, even when it's uncomfortable.

When people feel safe, they don't just stay — they thrive. And when they thrive, so does the organization.

Servistry teaches us that trust is not a luxury in leadership; it is the foundation. When we serve with intentionality, we create spaces where people feel seen, heard, and valued. That is the true measure of leadership. When leaders build trust and psychological safety, their influence extends beyond immediate teams. The culture they create reverberates throughout the organization and beyond.

CHAPTER TEN

THE RIPPLE EFFECT OF LEADERSHIP

I once heard a story about a small café nestled in a bustling city. The owner, a middle-aged man with salt-and-pepper hair, made it a habit to greet every customer with genuine warmth. He remembered names, asked about their families, and made sure no one ever felt like just another order on a receipt.

But it wasn't only the customers who noticed. His staff did too. They saw how he offered words of encouragement on hard days and celebrated their successes, big or small. Over time, they began mirroring his approach. Baristas learned regulars' favorite drinks by heart. The kitchen staff went the extra mile to plate dishes with care. And customers, in turn, began treating each other with the same kindness.

What started as a simple gesture of leadership rippled outward, touching people who had never even met the café owner.

That's the ripple effect of Servistry.

The Unseen Impact of Leadership

Leaders often underestimate the weight of their presence. A single decision, a moment of kindness, or a response in the face of failure can cascade through an organization, leaving echoes long after it's forgotten. But the same is true for moments of neglect — when feedback is dismissed, when contributions go unrecognized, or when fear seeps into the workplace.

Servistry teaches us that leadership isn't confined to titles or positions. It's an energy we release into the world. Every choice we make — how we treat a frustrated colleague, how we respond to difficult feedback, how we show up when no one is watching — sends ripples far beyond our immediate circle.

And those ripples don't stop at the office door.

When Leaders Serve, Teams Rise

I recall a time when a project I led had gone off track. Deadlines were slipping, tensions were rising, and the room felt heavier with each passing day. It would have been easy to shift blame or tighten control. But something told me to pause.

Instead, I gathered the team and asked one question:

"How can I help?"

The response wasn't immediate. Silence lingered. But then, one person spoke up about a process bottleneck they had been too hesitant to mention. Another shared that they were overwhelmed but didn't want to appear incapable. One by one, truths emerged — not as accusations, but as invitations for collective problem-solving.

I learned that day that Servistry is not about rescuing. It's about revealing. When we serve, we create space for people to step forward, own their challenges, and contribute their best. And when teams feel supported rather than scrutinized, they rise.

The ripple effect was unmistakable. Collaboration strengthened. Problem-solving became proactive. And eventually, we not only recovered but exceeded expectations. But the real victory? People no longer saw challenges as threats. They saw them as opportunities to grow.

From Teams to Customers

The most customer-centric organizations I've worked with often share one defining trait — they treat their employees with the same care they expect to offer their customers.

It's not just a matter of satisfaction surveys or quarterly bonuses. It's about whether people feel empowered to make decisions in service of the customer. I've seen frontline employees solve problems creatively because they knew their leaders trusted them. I've watched customer service representatives turn difficult calls into opportunities for connection because they felt valued themselves.

Servistry, when embedded into a team's culture, becomes visible to the outside world. Customers may not know the names of the leaders behind the scenes, but they feel the difference. They experience it in the extra effort, the thoughtful follow-up, the sincerity in an apology when things go wrong.

And just like that café owner's kindness, the ripple moves outward — from the leader to the employee, from the employee to the customer, and from the customer to the community.

The Ripple Beyond Business

There's a profound truth I've come to believe: *who we are at work is rarely confined to the walls of our office.*

I've seen leaders who embraced Servistry carry that same spirit into their communities. A manager who mentored a struggling employee found himself volunteering at a youth mentorship program. A CEO who prioritized psychological safety at work began fostering open conversations at home. A frontline supervisor who encouraged collaboration at work started coaching their child's soccer team with the same spirit of empowerment.

The ripple doesn't end when the workday does. Servistry becomes a way of living — one that shapes how we show up in every space we occupy.

Consider this:

- *Think of a leader who positively impacted you. How did their actions influence your own approach to leadership?*
- *Now think of a time when someone's negative leadership left a lasting impression. How did that experience shape your confidence, your voice, or your choices?*
- *Finally, ask yourself: What kind of ripple am I creating today?*

Servistry challenges us to lead not for the sake of recognition, but because we understand that our actions leave footprints — on people, on teams, and on the world around us.

There's something humbling about knowing that we may never see the full extent of our impact. The café owner likely never knew how many acts of kindness his leadership inspired. And perhaps I will never fully know how a single decision I made affected the course of someone else's journey.

But that's the beauty of the ripple effect. It moves quietly, carried forward by the people we touch, long after we've stepped away.

And as leaders committed to Servistry, that is more than enough. The most profound ripple begins within your own organization. As leaders, the service we extend to our employees directly shapes the culture we build.

CHAPTER ELEVEN

EMPLOYEE-CENTRIC LEADERSHIP

A Morning That Changed My Perspective

There was a time, early in my leadership journey, when I believed that my primary responsibility was to manage outcomes. I measured success by metrics — productivity, efficiency, bottom-line results. And while the numbers often painted a picture of success, something was missing.

It became clear one morning when a talented employee — let's call her Ananya — walked into my office with a resignation letter. I was stunned. She was one of our best performers, someone I had quietly labelled a "high potential."

"Why?" I asked, genuinely perplexed.

She hesitated. "I don't think I matter here," she said.

That line stayed with me. I'd spent so much time measuring output that I'd overlooked something essential — how people felt within the organization. Ananya didn't lack opportunity. She lacked a sense of being valued.

That day, I learned the difference between managing people and leading them. Servistry is built on the latter. And at its core is one undeniable truth — people who feel valued and empowered create the most enduring success.

Why Employee-Centric Leadership Matters

When leaders lead with Servistry, employees are not just a means to an end. They are the heart of the organization. Valuing people is not about grand gestures or performance-based rewards. It's about how leaders make employees feel in the moments that matter — in successes, setbacks, and everything in between.

Employee-centric leadership creates:

- *Trust: When people feel seen and heard, they reciprocate with commitment and dedication.*
  Sustained Performance: Teams that feel psychologically safe consistently outperform those that operate under fear or pressure.
- *Innovation: Empowered employees think creatively without the fear of failure.*
- *Loyalty: People don't leave organizations; they leave environments where they feel undervalued.*

The ripple effect of this leadership style extends far beyond the workplace. People who feel valued carry that sense of worth into their homes, communities, and future roles.

The Currency of Recognition

One of the simplest yet most powerful ways to create a people-first culture is through recognition. But meaningful recognition goes beyond routine "employee of the month" awards.

I recall a colleague named Raj, who led a small operations team. Despite the lack of visibility his team received, Raj ensured every milestone was celebrated. He personalized acknowledgments, not just praising outcomes but recognizing effort, resilience, and growth. Over time, people naturally gravitated toward Raj, not just because he was competent but because he saw them.

Recognition doesn't always require formal programs. A handwritten note, a few words of appreciation in a meeting, or even a public acknowledgment on a difficult day can fuel a person's sense of belonging. And often, those small moments are remembered far longer than any performance bonus.

Empowerment Through Ownership

Servistry thrives when leaders shift from directing to empowering. I once worked with a senior manager who believed his role was to approve every decision — from large investments to minor operational choices. His team grew increasingly dependent, hesitant to take initiative without his blessing. While he thought he was ensuring control, he was unknowingly stifling innovation.

When he finally embraced Servistry, he took a different approach. He started asking, "What do you think is the best course of action?" instead of, "Here's what I want you to do."

The shift was palpable. Decision-making accelerated. Employees gained confidence. And he found himself spending less time extinguishing fires and more time fostering growth.

Empowerment doesn't mean leaders disappear. It means they create environments where people feel trusted to make decisions, own outcomes, and learn from experiences. Servistry leaders are not just safety nets; they are trampolines — launching people upward.

Creating Moments That Matter

Leadership is often defined in the smallest moments.

There was a time when a young team member presented a new idea during a leadership meeting. It wasn't polished, and she stumbled through parts of her pitch. I could see the doubt creeping in. But instead of dismissing her, the leader in the room asked a simple question:

"What inspired you to come up with this idea?"

That moment shifted everything. Encouragement, not criticism, became the tone. The idea was refined and later became a successful project. More importantly, the young leader grew in confidence and continued contributing fearlessly.

Servistry means intentionally creating these moments. It means pausing long enough to ask, "How can I support you?" rather than rushing to correct. It means celebrating progress, not just perfection. And it means making sure people leave interactions feeling stronger than before.

As leaders, we often get consumed by what we deliver. But Servistry asks us to pause and consider:

- *Do my employees feel valued beyond their performance metrics?*
- *When was the last time I recognized someone's effort in a meaningful way?*
- *Am I empowering people to make decisions, or am I holding onto control?*
- *How often do I create opportunities for my team to grow and take ownership?*

The answers to these questions are often reflected in the culture we build. Servistry leaders recognize that every choice, no matter how small, shapes the experience of those they lead.

The Ananya Moment

Coming back to Ananya, I did what I should have done long before that resignation letter appeared. I listened. I apologised. And I committed to being better.

While Ananya eventually moved on, that conversation changed how I approached leadership. I realized that numbers are fleeting, but the impact we leave on people lasts far longer.

And perhaps, somewhere out there, Ananya carried forward that same belief — that she, too, could lead with Servistry. Because when we choose to serve our people, the ripple always continues.

As we reflect on what it means to be an employee-centric leader, it's clear that the greatest service we offer is creating an environment where people feel valued, empowered, and inspired. This doesn't come from policies or perks alone — it comes from genuine care and intentional leadership.

But centric leadership doesn't end with employees. When people feel deeply valued, their sense of ownership grows. They become not just contributors but champions — driving innovation, supporting one another, and naturally extending their service outward.

This brings us to an essential realization — employees and customers are not separate worlds. When you lead with people at the centre, the ripple effect reaches far beyond your organization. Up next, we'll explore how Servistry extends that same intentional care to the very people you serve — your customers. After all, just as empowered employees create exceptional workplaces, they also create exceptional customer experiences.

When leaders prioritize their people, those employees naturally carry the spirit of Servistry into their work. This impact is most visible in customer relationships.

CHAPTER TWELVE

CUSTOMERS AS STAKEHOLDERS

The Day I Lost a Customer

I remember the call vividly. A long-term client — one we considered part of our extended family — informed us they were ending the partnership. The reason? Not pricing, not competition, but something far more concerning.

"We didn't feel valued," they said.

It wasn't easy to hear. We'd delivered on deadlines, ensured product quality, and maintained professional communication. But somewhere in the race to achieve outcomes, we'd lost sight of what mattered — the relationship.

That day, I realized that businesses often call customers their "stakeholders" without truly treating them as such. A stakeholder isn't just someone who pays for a service. They are an active participant in the ecosystem — their voice, trust, and loyalty have the power to shape our success.

Servistry demands that we view customers not as transactions but as relationships. And when we lead with service, the results naturally follow.

The Customer-Service Paradox

It's easy to believe that excellent service is a cost — a resource drain with no immediate return. But I've found the opposite to be true. Organizations that embed service into their DNA see a compounding effect — not only in customer retention but in revenue growth, reputation, and resilience.

Think of service not as a reactive function but as a growth strategy. When customers feel valued, they don't just stay — they become advocates. They bring referrals, offer insights for innovation, and often grow their partnerships over time.

In a world of limitless choices, the most powerful competitive advantage is a relationship built on trust and care.

From Vendor to Partner

There's a stark difference between a vendor and a partner. Vendors deliver on contracts; partners invest in shared success. Servistry teaches us to shift our mindset from fulfilling obligations to creating value.

One of the most profound lessons I learned was from a client who faced a sudden crisis. Their market conditions changed overnight, and they needed flexibility to survive. Legally, we were under no obligation to adjust terms. But we did.

We waived fees, extended timelines, and supported them through uncertainty. That single decision, made from a place of service rather than self-interest, not only saved their business but deepened our partnership. Years later, they expanded their collaboration with us — not out of necessity but out of trust.

Servistry leaders understand that the returns on service are rarely immediate, but they are always enduring.

Listening Beyond Feedback

Many companies pride themselves on gathering customer feedback. Surveys, Net Promoter Scores, and satisfaction ratings fill executive dashboards. Yet, feedback without action is simply noise.

I've sat in countless meetings where feedback was acknowledged but rarely acted upon. Servistry demands that we go beyond passive listening. It asks us to approach feedback with curiosity, humility, and a willingness to change.

I recall a moment when a client pointed out a consistent gap in our service model. Instead of defending our processes, we invited them to collaborate on a solution. What emerged wasn't just a better service offering but a long-term alliance. They felt heard. And in return, they championed our brand to others.

Listening, when done with intent, is one of the most powerful acts of service.

Empathy at Scale

"Empathy" is often considered a personal trait — something leaders practice one-on-one. But can organizations practice empathy at scale? Absolutely.

Some companies excel at understanding the emotional needs of their customers. Think about the brands that remember your preferences, anticipate your needs, and resolve issues without friction. That's not just good service; that's Servistry in action.

Empathy at scale means:

- *Designing processes that reduce frustration, not create it.*
- *Training frontline teams to listen first, act second.*
- *Empowering employees to resolve problems without excessive escalation.*
- *Acknowledging mistakes and making them right — visibly and sincerely.*

A customer who experiences empathy doesn't forget it. And in an era of commoditized products and services, that emotional connection becomes the greatest differentiator.

When Service Fuels Growth

There's a reason companies with a reputation for exceptional service consistently outperform their competitors. Their growth isn't just a result of marketing or innovation — it's the byproduct of trust.

Consider how often we recommend brands not because of their product features, but because of how they made us feel. That's the ripple effect of Servistry.

I've seen organizations grow exponentially simply by doubling down on service. A hospitality brand that empowered its staff to make on-the-spot decisions for guest satisfaction. A financial firm that proactively advised clients on managing market volatility. A logistics company that prioritized transparency over convenience when supply chain issues arose. }

In every case, service wasn't a line item — it was the growth strategy.

As you think about your own leadership and the role service plays in your business, ask yourself:

- *Do we see customers as stakeholders or as transactions?*
- *How often do we proactively engage with customers, not just to sell, but to understand?*
- *Are we willing to serve even when it isn't immediately profitable?*
- *Do our employees feel empowered to prioritize service without fear of reprimand?*
- *When a customer leaves, do we reflect on what we could have done differently?*

These questions are not easy. But Servistry requires us to sit with discomfort, own our gaps, and choose service anyway.

The Client Who Returned

Months after we lost that client, I received a call from them again. Not to reopen the partnership, but to share that they'd applied the same service-first approach in their own organization.

"Your loss was our lesson," they said.

And perhaps, it was mine too.

Because Servistry isn't just about gaining customers — it's about earning the privilege to serve them. And sometimes, the greatest growth happens not in victory, but in reflection.

Viewing customers as stakeholders is not a transactional mindset — it's a transformational one. Servistry challenges us to step beyond the conventional notions of customer satisfaction and into the realm of shared success.

When we align our goals with the needs of those we serve, loyalty becomes a natural outcome, not a pursued target.

But this concept doesn't live in isolation. Just as we serve our customers, we must continue to serve our people. The connection between employee satisfaction and customer satisfaction is inseparable. Empowered employees who feel supported and valued bring that same energy and dedication to customer relationships.

As we move forward, we'll shift our focus to the broader influence of leadership. Servistry's impact doesn't stop with customers — it cascades across teams, communities, and industries. In the next chapter, we'll explore how the ripple effect of service-oriented leadership transforms organizations from the inside out.

Phase – III

Mastery of Servistry

CHAPTER THIRTEEN

DEVELOPING FUTURE LEADERS

A Personal Reflection: Passing the Torch

I remember the first time I was tasked with mentoring a young leader. At the time, I saw leadership development as a simple knowledge transfer — teaching what I knew and hoping they would apply it. But the experience was far from linear.

It wasn't just about sharing insights; it was about holding space for growth, navigating uncertainties together, and trusting them to find their voice. What I didn't realize then was that leadership isn't taught — it's unlocked. And unlocking leadership requires a mindset rooted in service.

This is where Servistry comes into play. Developing future leaders through Servistry means fostering capability, courage, and character — not just competence. It's about nurturing leaders who act with intention, prioritize people, and create a ripple effect of positive influence.

Why Developing Future Leaders Matters

Organizations often focus on identifying high potentials or implementing leadership programs. While these initiatives are valuable, they sometimes miss the essence of what makes leadership thrive. True leadership development isn't a checklist — it's a shared commitment to growth, one that multiplies over time.

Consider this: Every leader we nurture extends the principles of Servistry to their teams, customers, and stakeholders. The impact transcends individual actions. Leaders who embody service-led leadership contribute to cultures where people feel empowered, valued, and inspired to lead themselves.

The Servistry Approach to Leadership Development

Teaching Servistry across leadership levels means embracing three core principles:

1. Lead Through Example

Leadership development starts with us. Future leaders don't just listen to what we say — they observe how we lead. When we demonstrate empathy, decisiveness, and resilience, it sets a powerful standard. Servistry invites us to ask:

- *Am I modelling the behaviours I wish to see in future leaders?*
- *How can my choices reflect service to both people and purpose?*

2. Empower Autonomy, Not Dependency

Early in my leadership journey, I thought supporting others meant providing solutions. Over time, I learned that true support is about asking the right questions, encouraging ownership, and trusting people's decisions. Servistry-based development creates leaders who think critically and act confidently.

- *Where can I step back to create space for others to lead?*
- *Am I fostering self-reliance or dependence?*

3. Create Psychological Safety for Growth

Growth is rarely comfortable. It often involves navigating uncertainty, making mistakes, and facing setbacks. Leaders practicing Servistry understand this and intentionally create environments where people feel safe to experiment and learn.

- *How do I respond when mistakes happen?*
- *Am I encouraging a culture of learning or one of fear?*

A Story of Leadership in Action

A few years ago, I worked with a mid-level manager named Riya. She was ambitious, talented, and eager to grow. But despite her potential, she hesitated to take bold decisions. Fear of failure held her back.

Instead of offering quick solutions, I chose to apply Servistry. I gave her ownership of a critical project, assuring her that I trusted her judgment. When challenges arose, I resisted the temptation to step in. Instead, I encouraged her to analyse, reflect, and choose her path.

The transformation was remarkable. Riya not only delivered the project successfully but also emerged as a confident, decisive leader. What stayed with me was what she said later:

"You didn't just teach me leadership; you helped me see it within myself."

This is the essence of Servistry. Leadership is not imposed — it's uncovered.

Teaching Servistry at Different Levels

Leadership development is not a one-size-fits-all approach. As we guide individuals across different leadership levels, Servistry adapts to meet their evolving needs.

- **First-Time Leaders**: Focus on building self-awareness and developing foundational leadership habits. Encourage them to lead with empathy and integrity.
- **Mid-Level Leaders**: Shift the focus toward influencing without authority, coaching others, and driving impact across teams. Servistry here is about balancing results with people-centricity.
- **Senior Leaders**: Guide them in shaping culture, making strategic decisions, and mentoring the next generation. At this level, leaders become stewards of Servistry, multiplying its impact across the organization.

Reflection for Leaders: Are You Multiplying Leadership?

Pause for a moment and consider:

- *Who are the emerging leaders you're investing in today?*
- *How are you modelling the principles of Servistry in your daily leadership?*
- *Are you building leaders who serve with purpose, courage, and compassion?*

True leadership development isn't about cloning ourselves. It's about empowering others to lead in their own authentic way. When we practice Servistry, we create leaders who, in turn, create leaders — forming a legacy of service that outlasts our individual contributions.

The best leaders I've known didn't just achieve business results. They inspired, empowered, and left behind stronger organizations and people. They understood that leadership isn't a title — it's a responsibility.

As you continue your journey of Servistry, remember this: The future of leadership isn't shaped by policies or programs. It's shaped by the choices we make every day. And when we choose to lead with a
service mindset, we create a ripple effect that transcends ourselves.

CHAPTER FOURTEEN

SCALING SERVICE IN LARGE

There's a unique challenge that every leader faces as their responsibilities grow. When you lead a small team, you can personally engage with each person, understand their challenges, and influence the culture with direct actions. But what happens when that team turns into hundreds, or even thousands, spread across different locations?

The question is no longer just about how you lead — it's about how you make leadership felt. And that's where Servistry steps in.

A Moment of Realization

I remember walking into a large manufacturing plant during one of my early leadership roles. Rows of machines buzzed, people moved with urgency, and leaders monitored dashboards tracking the day's productivity. Amid the operational intensity, I noticed something unsettling — people were present, but not fully engaged. The spark I'd seen in smaller teams, where conversations flowed freely and challenges were tackled together, seemed missing.

The truth was that decisions made at the top felt distant on the factory floor. Policies trickled down without context, and middle managers carried the burden of translating directives into action. It wasn't a lack of effort; it was a lack of connection.

That's when I understood — scaling Servistry wasn't about broadcasting values from the top. It was about empowering leaders at every level to embody those values, making service a lived experience rather than a corporate statement.

Why Scaling Service Matters

The ripple effect of leadership is undeniable. When leaders lead with service, it's contagious. People feel valued, seen, and supported. Decisions become more thoughtful, innovation flourishes, and loyalty deepens — not just from employees, but from customers and communities.

But without intentionality, scale can dilute purpose. The larger an organization becomes, the easier it is for the essence of Servistry to get lost in processes, policies, and numbers. That's why organizations need to design for service.

Scaling Servistry means creating a culture where service is self-sustaining — where the intent to serve remains alive no matter how large the organization grows.

How Servistry Grows at Scale

A leader's role evolves as the organization expands. While personal influence may diminish, their ability to shape the environment grows exponentially. Here's how Servistry flourishes when scaled effectively:

1. Leaders as Multipliers, Not Controllers

In large organizations, the temptation to control every outcome is real. I've been there — feeling the pressure to monitor, approve, and oversee every decision. But true service-led leadership means multiplying leadership, not hoarding it.

I once worked with a regional manager who embodied this perfectly. Rather than micromanaging store-level decisions, he empowered local leaders to innovate. He encouraged them to find solutions that suited their specific communities. When a problem arose, his first question wasn't, "Why did this happen?" but "How can I help you solve this?" The result? Ownership increased, and so did customer satisfaction.

Scaling Servistry requires trust — believing that when people are aligned with a shared purpose, they will act in the organization's best interest.

Reflection:

- *Where can you relinquish control to empower others?*
- *Are your leaders equipped to make service-led decisions?*

2. Systems that Sustain Service

Culture cannot survive on good intentions alone. I've seen organizations with inspiring mission statements fail to live up to them because their systems didn't support service. Performance metrics that prioritize numbers over people, rigid policies that stifle innovation, and hierarchical decision-making all undermine Servistry.

One organization I admire introduced a concept called "Service Councils." These cross-functional groups regularly reviewed how company policies impacted frontline employees and customers. If something hindered service, the council had the authority to recommend changes. It wasn't about breaking rules — it was about removing unnecessary obstacles.

Reflection:

- *Are your policies and systems reinforcing service or hindering it?*
- *How often do frontline perspectives shape leadership decisions?*

3. Stories that Spread the Message

Data may measure success, but stories inspire action. I vividly recall a time when an employee at a logistics company went beyond their role to hand-deliver an urgent medical shipment after hours. That story traveled across the organization, reinforcing the belief that people mattered more than policies

Leaders can amplify Servistry by celebrating stories of service. Not just grand gestures, but everyday moments of kindness, problem-solving, and collaboration. Stories humanize leadership, making it relatable and actionable.

Reflection:

- *What service stories are circulating in your organization?*
- *How can you create opportunities to share and celebrate them?*

The Road Ahead

Scaling Servistry isn't a one-time initiative. It's a mindset shift that requires constant nurturing. The beauty of Servistry is that it evolves — as leaders grow, as organizations expand, and as challenges change.

As you reflect on your leadership journey, consider this:

- *Are you building systems that enable service rather than control it?*
- *Are you empowering others to lead with purpose and act with empathy?*
- *Are stories of service celebrated and used to inspire future decisions?*
- Scaling Servistry isn't about replicating leadership — it's about multiplying it. It's about creating an environment where every leader, at every level, feels empowered to lead with purpose and serve those around them.

When leaders scale service, they don't just grow organizations; they grow people. And that growth leaves a legacy — one that extends far beyond individual achievements, shaping a future where leadership is defined not by authority, but by service.

And when Servistry scales, it becomes more than a leadership philosophy. It becomes the foundation of how organizations operate — resilient, people-centered, and purpose-driven. And in that, both leaders and organizations leave a legacy that endures.

CHAPTER FIFTEEN

Servistry and Innovation

Innovation is often romanticized as the domain of visionaries — people with extraordinary ideas that disrupt industries and redefine the future. But for most leaders, innovation isn't born in isolation or grand moments of inspiration. It grows from a continuous commitment to serve. When leaders lead with a service-first mindset, innovation ceases to be a pursuit of novelty. It becomes a response — a responsibility — to make life better for those we serve.

I learned this not through a course or a strategy session but in a moment of failure.

When Service Redefined the Problem

Years ago, I was part of a leadership team in an organization that prided itself on being customer-centric. Despite our efforts, customer satisfaction scores were stagnating. We were convinced that what we needed was a bold, innovative solution — perhaps a technological leap or a revamped service offering.

We brought in consultants, reviewed market trends, and analysed every competitor's move. But the more we searched for external inspiration, the further we drifted from the people we were trying to serve.

One afternoon, after hours of discussions, a senior colleague quietly asked, "When was the last time we truly listened to our customers — not just through surveys, but by walking in their shoes?"

That question shifted everything.

Instead of pursuing innovation as a product, we pursued it as a perspective. We spent weeks visiting branches, listening to employees on the frontlines, and engaging with customers who voiced frustrations, hopes, and even suggestions. What we heard was humbling. It wasn't the lack of technology or complex service gaps causing dissatisfaction — it was the absence of care.

A service representative summed it up perfectly:

"I follow processes, but I rarely get the chance to solve problems the way I know I should. The rules often come before the relationship."

Innovation didn't begin with a brainstorming session. It began when we removed the fear of failure from employees, encouraged them to challenge rigid policies, and empowered them to serve with autonomy. Small, thoughtful changes — like giving frontline teams greater decision-making authority — transformed customer experiences.

That wasn't just problem-solving. That was innovation.

Innovation Through Empathy

Looking back, I realize that the most enduring innovations come not from a desire to be different, but from the desire to serve better. Leaders who practice Servistry instinctively ask: What are we missing? How can we make this easier, kinder, or more valuable for others?

I recall a healthcare leader who faced a similar challenge. Patients complained about the long and confusing discharge process, and leadership initially assumed a technological solution would resolve it. But when they took the time to observe the experience from the patient's perspective, they saw something no system could fix — the emotional toll of feeling forgotten.

The innovation that followed wasn't groundbreaking software. It was the creation of a "patient advocate" role — a dedicated team member who guided patients through the process with empathy and clarity. The impact was immediate. Patient satisfaction soared, not because the process was faster, but because people felt seen and supported.

That's the essence of Servistry. When leaders see service as an opportunity to innovate, they move beyond surface-level improvements. They dig deeper into the human experience. And in doing so, they uncover possibilities no market analysis could reveal.

Creating a Culture of Innovation

Service-driven innovation is not about grand gestures. It is about creating the conditions where ideas are welcomed, explored, and embraced. In organizations where Servistry thrives, failure is not seen as a threat. It is seen as a teacher.

A global hospitality company I once worked with embraced this mindset wholeheartedly. Rather than relying solely on innovation teams, they empowered every employee — from housekeeping staff to chefs — to suggest improvements. Leadership ensured that every idea, no matter how small, was acknowledged and explored.

The most celebrated idea that year didn't come from the executive floor. It came from a front-desk associate who noticed how often families requested nearby dining recommendations. Instead of providing generic brochures, the hotel created a personalized digital map with curated recommendations from local staff. Guests loved it, and it quickly became a brand signature.

No complex algorithms. No disruptive technology. Just a simple act of service that turned into a competitive advantage.

The Courage to Stay Curious

Servistry demands curiosity — the willingness to question why things are done a certain way and whether they could be done better. It takes courage to challenge tradition, especially when the systems in place seem to be working well enough.

But as I've seen time and time again, "well enough" is the enemy of great leadership.

There's a distinct moment in the journey of every service-led leader when they realize that innovation is not about proving brilliance. It's about proving care. Care for employees who deserve to feel empowered. Care for customers who deserve experiences that delight, not frustrate. Care for communities that benefit when organizations act with purpose.

In Servistry, the most powerful question a leader can ask is not, "What's the next big thing?" It's "How can we serve better?"

And if you listen closely enough, the answer is always waiting.

CHAPTER SIXTEEN

LEADING IN CRISIS

Servistry as a Framework for Resilience.

A crisis tests everything we know about leadership. It strips away the layers of strategy and vision, leaving us face-to-face with uncertainty. But in that uncertainty, the essence of leadership reveals itself. Servistry — leading through service — becomes both a compass and a lifeline.

A Crisis of My Own

I vividly recall one particular crisis that shook the foundation of my leadership. A sudden economic downturn had left our company in a vulnerable position. Revenue was plummeting, layoffs were looming, and fear echoed through the hallways. As leaders, we faced difficult choices — the kind that keep you awake at night.

In one moment, I was a decision-maker. In the next, I was the bearer of bad news. But through it all, I remember one thought anchoring me: How can I serve my people, even when I can't promise certainty?

That question changed everything. It shifted my focus from damage control to people care. I couldn't control the external factors, but I could control how I showed up — with honesty, compassion, and unwavering presence. Servistry demanded that I lead not from a place of authority, but from a place of empathy.

Choosing Transparency Over Perfection

In times of crisis, the instinct to shield people from the harsh truth can be strong. I've been there. But I've also learned that withholding transparency breeds fear. When we pretend to have all the answers, we create distance.

I remember standing before my team, their eyes filled with concern. I didn't have reassuring figures to share. What I had was honesty. I told them what I knew, what I didn't, and what we were committed to figuring out — together. The room, once tense, softened. Fear didn't disappear, but trust began to take its place.

Transparency is an act of service. It doesn't mean providing false hope; it means respecting people enough to involve them in the reality of the moment.

The Weight of Leadership

Leadership in crisis is lonely. Even with the best advisors and support systems, the burden feels deeply personal. I carried the weight of every decision — knowing that livelihoods, families, and futures were at stake.

But Servistry reminded me that leadership is not about bearing the weight alone. It's about inviting others to share the load. One of the most humbling moments I experienced was when a frontline employee, someone I rarely interacted with, approached me after a town hall. "Thank you for not pretending," she said. "It helps to know we're in this together."

That exchange stayed with me. It reminded me that resilience is not built in isolation. It's forged in the collective strength of a team that feels seen and heard.

Service in the Hardest Moments

During that crisis, decisions had to be made — some of them painful. Roles were eliminated, and the weight of those choices lingered. Servistry didn't mean avoiding those decisions; it meant making them with dignity and care.

We ensured every departing employee was treated with respect, provided resources, and supported through their transition. It wasn't perfect. It never is. But the commitment to serve extended even to those we had to let go.

And for those who remained, the message was clear: Your well-being matters. Your voice matters. We will rebuild together.

Emerging Stronger

Eventually, the storm passed. The business recovered, but more importantly, the culture endured. People remembered how they were treated when things were at their worst. Trust wasn't just restored — it was strengthened.

Servistry doesn't offer immunity from crisis. It offers resilience. It teaches us that even in the darkest moments, our leadership is measured not by the certainty we project, but by the care we provide.

A Question for Every Leader

The next time you find yourself in the heart of a crisis, pause and ask:

How can I serve?

Because when service becomes your guiding principle, you'll find clarity where confusion once reigned. And in that clarity, you'll lead not just through the storm — but beyond it.

CHAPTER SEVENTEEN

BALANCING SERVICE & RESULTS

I remember a time when I thought being a good leader meant saying "yes" to everything. Every request, every challenge, every opportunity — I welcomed it all. I thought it was a reflection of my commitment to serve. After all, wasn't that what leadership was about? Being available, responsive, and unwavering?

But that version of leadership has a cost — one that too many leaders, myself included, know all too well. The calendar fills. The days stretch. The inbox overflows. Slowly, the passion that once fuelled the desire to serve turns into exhaustion. And when exhaustion sets in, so does doubt.

It took me a while to understand that true service isn't about giving endlessly until there's nothing left. It's about giving meaningfully, in a way that sustains both yourself and the people you lead. Servistry, in its essence, is not a demand for sacrifice. It's a call for balance — aligning service with results, without tipping into burnout.

When Service Becomes a Strain

I recall a particular phase in my career when I was leading a large, cross-functional team during a major business transformation. The stakes were high, and the expectation to deliver results weighed heavily. I wanted to be the leader my team could count on — the one who always showed up, no matter how challenging the day.

At first, I thrived on the sense of purpose. But as the weeks went on, I started noticing the signs — the sleepless nights, the short fuse, the growing resentment toward tasks I once found fulfilling. I brushed it off, thinking resilience meant pushing through.

Then, one day, a colleague — someone I trusted deeply — pulled me aside. She didn't comment on the business metrics or the project timeline. She asked a simple question that struck harder than any performance review ever could:

"Are you okay?"

I wasn't. But that moment sparked a realization — I had been so consumed with serving others that I had neglected the one person I needed to serve first: myself.

The Misconception of Service as Self-Sacrifice

There's a common belief that service and self-sacrifice are two sides of the same coin. Leaders are often celebrated for their dedication, their long hours, their relentless drive. But Servistry challenges this notion.

Service, in its most powerful form, isn't about depletion — it's about sustenance. When we lead with Servistry, we recognize that our well-being directly influences our ability to lead effectively. A burnt-out leader cannot serve at their best.

I've come to believe that the most sustainable leaders are those who:

- ***Prioritize Their Energy***: *They know when to step forward and when to step back.*
- ***Empower Others***: *They distribute leadership instead of hoarding it.*
- ***Measure Impact, Not Hours***: *They focus on results rather than the number of tasks they complete.*
- ***Listen to Themselves***: *They honor their limits, recognizing that resilience isn't about enduring — it's about recovering.*

A Shift in Perspective

The turning point for me came when I reframed the question. Instead of asking, "How much more can I do?" I started asking, "How can I create the most impact without sacrificing my well-being?"

This shift wasn't immediate, and it wasn't always comfortable. Setting boundaries felt foreign at first. Saying "no" — especially when I believed it might disappoint someone — went against everything I thought leadership required.

But something unexpected happened. The more I focused on sustainable leadership, the stronger my service became.

I began to delegate with intention, not as a means of relinquishing responsibility, but as a way to develop others. My team grew more confident, empowered to make decisions without constant oversight. I carved out time for strategic thinking — the kind of work that often gets buried under the urgency of the day.

And perhaps most importantly, I rediscovered the joy of leading.

The Ripple Effect of Sustainable Leadership

The impact wasn't limited to my own well-being. My team thrived. They saw a leader who modeled balance — someone who valued both results and relationships. And that gave them permission to do the same.

I once had a team member who approached me, reflecting on how the shift in leadership had changed her perspective. "I used to think success meant burnout," she admitted. "But now I see that it's possible to achieve more without sacrificing everything in the process."

That's Servistry in action. It's not about choosing between service and results. It's about recognizing that when we serve sustainably, we achieve both.

Embracing Servistry Without Burnout

If you find yourself at that same crossroads — torn between the desire to serve and the fear of burnout — I offer this:

1. Redefine What Service Means

Service isn't about being indispensable. It's about empowering others to thrive. When you create opportunities for growth, you multiply your impact.

2. Protect Your Energy as a Leadership Asset

Schedule time for what fuels you — whether it's reflection, exercise, or moments of quiet. Your energy is one of your most valuable resources. Treat it accordingly.

3. Lead Through Clarity, Not Chaos

Align your priorities with purpose. Not everything urgent is important. Servistry requires discernment — knowing when to engage deeply and when to step back.

4. Model Sustainable Leadership

Your team will mirror what you practice. When they see you value balance, well-being, and intentional service, they'll follow suit.

The leader I am today is not the one who tried to serve by doing it all. The leader I am today is one who understands that sustainable service isn't a compromise. It's a choice — one that allows both leaders and those they serve to flourish.

So as you navigate the demands of leadership, remember this: You serve best when you lead sustainably.

And when you do, the ripple effect is undeniable.

CHAPTER EIGHTEEN

ETHICAL LEADERSHIP AND INTEGRITY

I once heard someone say that integrity is what we do when no one is watching. It struck me then, but as I've grown in my leadership journey, I've come to believe that integrity is also what we do when everyone is watching.

In moments of challenge, when the easier path presents itself, ethical leadership is the choice to stay true to our values — not because it is convenient, but because it is right. And in the world of Servistry, where leadership is centered on serving others, integrity becomes the compass that ensures we never lose our way.

When Values Are Tested

I remember a particular incident early in my leadership career. We were in the final stages of a high-stakes project, and an unexpected setback threatened to delay our timeline. Tensions ran high, and the pressure to find a quick fix mounted.

A suggestion surfaced — one that was technically legal, but ethically questionable. It would allow us to meet the deadline, but at the cost of compromising transparency with our stakeholders. I found myself at a crossroads. The temptation to justify the decision was real. After all, wouldn't we be serving the organization's goals by delivering on time?

But that's when I realized something fundamental: Service without integrity isn't service at all. It's self-preservation masked as leadership.

I chose to address the issue openly. I gathered the team, explained the challenge, and we explored alternative solutions. It wasn't easy. The project faced a minor delay, but we delivered without compromising our principles. What I didn't expect was the level of respect and trust it built — not only with my team but with our stakeholders.

That moment reminded me that ethical leadership isn't always about avoiding difficult decisions; it's about facing them with courage and clarity.

The Moral Responsibility of Leaders

When we adopt Servistry as our leadership philosophy, we acknowledge a deeper responsibility. Our decisions don't just affect the bottom line — they influence people's lives, their well-being, and the trust they place in us.

Ethical leadership requires us to hold ourselves accountable to three key principles:

1.Transparency: Leaders who serve are honest, even when the truth is uncomfortable. They communicate openly, ensuring their stakeholders understand the reasoning behind decisions.

2. Fairness: Serving others means valuing equity over expediency. Ethical leaders consider how their choices impact every individual, especially those who may lack a voice in the decision-making process.

3. Courage: It takes courage to stand up for what's right, particularly when it goes against popular opinion. Ethical leaders are willing to challenge the status quo and accept the consequences of their convictions.

I've come to see that these principles are not burdens; they are the very foundation of trust. And in leadership, trust is currency.

Integrity in the Face of Pressure

Pressure reveals character. When stakes are high, shortcuts become tempting, and rationalizations can cloud judgment. But ethical leaders understand that the long-term consequences of compromised integrity far outweigh the short-term gains.

I once worked alongside a leader known for his unwavering commitment to ethical decision-making. During a financial downturn, the company faced tough choices. Layoffs seemed inevitable, and the pressure to prioritize profits was immense. Yet instead of taking the easiest path, he chose a transparent approach.

He openly communicated with employees, explored cost-cutting measures, and even reduced executive bonuses to minimize the impact. Ultimately, fewer layoffs were required than anticipated. His decision wasn't just ethical — it was a demonstration of Servistry in action.

The loyalty and respect he earned through that decision far outweighed any financial gains that a more ruthless approach might have secured. It was a powerful reminder that ethical leadership doesn't sacrifice people for results; it finds a way to achieve both.

Creating an Ethical Culture

Leaders don't just practice integrity — they cultivate it. An ethical leader creates a ripple effect that influences the culture of the entire organization.

Here's how Servistry can guide leaders in embedding integrity into their teams and organizations:

- *Model the Behaviour: People learn more from what leaders do than from what they say. Consistently acting with integrity sets the standard for others.*
- *Create Psychological Safety: Encourage open dialogue. When employees feel safe to raise concerns without fear of retaliation, ethical issues are addressed early.*
- *Recognize Ethical Courage: Celebrate those who make principled decisions, even when it's inconvenient. This reinforces the message that doing what's right is valued.*
- *Establish Clear Values: Ethical cultures are built on clear, actionable values. Leaders must ensure these values are not just framed on walls but reflected in daily decisions.*
- *Stay Accountable: Ethical leaders invite feedback and remain open to scrutiny. They understand that accountability strengthens trust.*

The Inner Compass

Servistry reminds us that the most challenging decisions are often the most defining ones. Every time we choose integrity over expediency, we reinforce not only our leadership but also the trust others place in us.

If you ever find yourself questioning the right course of action, pause and reflect:

- Am I serving or self-serving?
- Would I stand by this decision if it were publicly known?
- Am I acting in alignment with the values I claim to uphold?

These questions are not easy. But that's the nature of ethical leadership — it demands self-awareness, humility, and the courage to choose integrity, even when it's inconvenient.

A Lasting Legacy

In the end, our leadership will not be remembered solely by the results we achieved, but by the manner in which we achieved them. Did we lead with integrity? Did we uplift others? Did we choose service over self-interest?

Servistry offers a simple yet profound reminder: The moral responsibility of serving others is not a burden — it's an honor. And when we embrace that responsibility, we don't just lead organizations. We inspire trust, we build legacies, and we create a world where leadership is a force for good.

That is the true essence of ethical leadership.

Phase – IV

Mastery of Servistry

CHAPTER NINETEEN

SERVISTRY LEADERSHIP MODEL

When we talk about leadership, most conversations revolve around results, influence, and strategy. But Servistry shifts that perspective. It starts with one simple question: How can I serve?

This chapter is about translating that question into action. Becoming a Servistry leader isn't about following a template — it's about understanding the essence of service, applying it with intention, and leading with impact.

Let me share how this transformation unfolds through the Servistry Leadership Model.

1. Understanding the Servistry Commitment

Becoming a Servistry leader begins with a commitment — not to titles or accolades, but to service as a defining principle. This mindset demands courage. It requires choosing people over convenience, conversations over control, and purpose over short-term wins.

I remember early in my career when I was tasked with leading a struggling division. The instinct was to impose quick fixes. But instead, I paused. I listened. I understood the frustrations of the frontline teams. What followed wasn't a turnaround driven by authority — it was one powered by empathy and shared purpose.

Commitment means:

- *Prioritizing people and purpose alongside results.*
- *Embracing the responsibility to serve your teams, customers, and stakeholders.*
- *Remaining accountable for both the process and the outcome.*

2. Shaping Self-Awareness and Emotional Mastery

The strongest Servistry leaders are deeply self-aware. They acknowledge their biases, regulate their emotions, and listen with humility. Emotional mastery isn't about suppressing feelings; it's about recognizing and understanding them to lead with clarity.

Think of a leader navigating a high-pressure negotiation. A Servistry leader acknowledges the tension, but instead of reacting defensively, they remain curious. "What's driving the other party's perspective?" That shift from reaction to reflection opens space for collaboration.

To practice self-awareness:

- *Seek feedback regularly — especially the uncomfortable kind.*
- *Reflect on your emotional triggers and how they shape your decisions.*
- *Commit to intentional pauses before reacting.*

3. Building a Service-First Vision

Leaders often set goals based solely on growth metrics. Servistry leaders, however, craft visions that answer a larger question: Who benefits when we succeed, and how?

When you align your vision with service, you naturally drive impact beyond the bottom line. Consider a healthcare leader striving not only for operational efficiency but also for dignified patient experiences. That's Servistry in action.

To build your service-first vision:

- *Identify the communities you serve — employees, customers, partners, and beyond.*
- *Define success through both tangible results and human impact.*
- *Communicate this vision with clarity and passion.*

4. Empowering Through Trust and Psychological Safety

True service means relinquishing control. It's about empowering others, trusting their judgment, and creating a space where voices are heard. Psychological safety becomes the foundation for innovation, resilience, and authentic collaboration.

I recall a manager I once worked with who made it a practice to ask, "What's your perspective?" before every major decision. That simple question empowered team members to challenge ideas and propose solutions — because they knew their voices mattered.

To foster psychological safety:

- *Welcome dissenting views and acknowledge mistakes as learning opportunities.*
- *Actively listen without judgment.*
- *Recognize and celebrate contributions, especially those that challenge the norm.*

5. Leading with Consistency and Integrity

In Servistry, leadership isn't situational. It's not about serving when it's convenient or when eyes are watching. Consistency — in decisions, behaviour, and values — defines your leadership credibility.

There was a time I faced immense pressure to compromise on ethical grounds to meet short-term goals. But Servistry reminded me that serving stakeholders includes protecting the long-term integrity of the organization. The harder choice became the right one.

To lead with integrity:

- *Align your actions with your stated values, even when it's difficult.*
- *Be transparent about challenges and decision-making processes.*
- *Hold yourself and others accountable.*

6. Sustaining Servistry — Leading the Next Generation

Leadership doesn't end with individual growth. Servistry leaders are committed to developing others — nurturing future leaders who will carry forward the mindset of service.

This means mentoring with intention, creating opportunities for others to lead, and celebrating their successes. In my experience, the most fulfilling leadership moments came not from personal achievements, but from watching those I mentored grow into impactful leaders themselves.

To sustain Servistry:

- *Offer mentorship that goes beyond career advice — focus on personal growth and purpose.*
- *Create learning spaces where emerging leaders can experiment, fail, and grow.*
- *Advocate for people-first leadership within and beyond your organization.*

The Continuous Path of Servistry:

Becoming a Servistry leader isn't a destination. It's a continuous path of growth, reflection, and intentional service. You'll face moments of doubt. You'll navigate resistance. But with each decision rooted in service, your impact will ripple far beyond what you can measure.

So, as you turn the page, I invite you to ask yourself:

Where can I serve today?

That question, simple as it may seem, has the power to transform your leadership — and the world around you.

CHAPTER TWENTY

MEASURING THE IMPACT OF SERVISTRY

Business and People Metrics Across Diverse Settings

Leadership is often measured by its results. However, when leadership is anchored in Servistry, the true measure of success goes beyond traditional financial outcomes. It encompasses the growth of people, the strength of relationships, and the overall health of an organization. The challenge, then, is to find ways to capture these outcomes — not only in large corporations but also in small businesses, startups, and non-corporate settings.

This chapter offers a flexible, inclusive approach to measuring the impact of Servistry, ensuring leaders at all levels and across industries can understand their progress and refine their leadership journey.

Why Measure Servistry?

Measuring the impact of Servistry isn't about rigid key performance indicators (KPIs). It's about gaining insights into the effectiveness of service-led leadership and its influence on people and organizations. Whether you lead a multinational organization, a local business, a nonprofit, or a community initiative, thoughtful measurement reveals the tangible effects of leading through service.

When applied effectively, Servistry metrics help to:

- Validate the effectiveness of leadership decisions
- Identify areas for growth and alignment
- Encourage a people-centered culture
- Align leadership efforts with long-term goals

1. People-Centric Metrics

At the heart of Servistry is people. How employees, customers, and stakeholders experience leadership directly reflects the quality of service being provided. Regardless of the setting, these are essential metrics to monitor:

A. Employee Engagement and Satisfaction

- In Corporations: Regular employee surveys, eNPS (Employee Net Promoter Score), and leadership effectiveness ratings.
- In Small Businesses: Informal feedback loops, one-on-one check-ins, and open team discussions.
- In Startups: Pulse surveys and retention analysis, particularly to assess alignment with the company's vision.
- In Non-Corporate Settings: Observing volunteer participation rates and gathering community feedback.

B. Psychological Safety and Trust

- Measurable Through: Trust index surveys, anonymous feedback platforms, or one-on-one conversations.
- Indicator: When employees feel safe to share ideas and admit mistakes without fear of repercussions, Servistry is thriving.

2. Business Performance Metrics

While Servistry is fundamentally about service, it also strengthens business outcomes. The following measures assess how well service-led leadership translates into financial and operational success:

A. Customer Satisfaction and Loyalty

- In Corporations: Net Promoter Score (NPS), Customer Satisfaction Score (CSAT), and churn rate.
- In Small Businesses: Customer referrals, repeat business, and reviews on platforms like Google or Yelp.
- In Startups: Feedback from early adopters, product-market fit surveys, and customer lifetime value.

B. Operational Efficiency

- In Corporations: Productivity KPIs, process improvement metrics, and employee turnover rates.
- In Small Businesses: Reduction in errors, improved order fulfilment times, or smoother customer experiences.
- In Startups: Time-to-market for new products, agility in adapting to feedback, and lean operational metrics.

3. Social and Community Impact Metrics

In Servistry, success is not solely measured within the organization. The impact on society and communities also matters. Leaders who serve with purpose often contribute to social well-being.

- In Corporations: Track CSR (Corporate Social Responsibility) impact, volunteer hours, and community engagement.
- In Small Businesses: Assess partnerships with local organizations, customer perceptions of social responsibility, and local employment impact.
- In Non-Corporate Settings: Evaluate community development milestones, participation in social causes, and qualitative feedback from beneficiaries.

4. Personal Leadership Growth Metrics

Servistry also invites self-assessment. Leaders should measure their growth by reflecting on their service mindset and leadership behaviours.

- In All Settings:
- Frequency of self-reflection and personal journaling
- Feedback from peers and mentors
- Ability to navigate challenging decisions with integrity
- Emotional intelligence and empathy growth
- Moments of resilience and learning from failure

Personal reflection is often the most overlooked yet profound form of measurement. As a leader practicing Servistry, asking yourself, "How have I served others this week?" can be as impactful as any external metric.

Integrating Servistry Metrics for Holistic Insight

While large corporations may rely on comprehensive dashboards and analytics, smaller businesses and non-corporate settings often benefit from simple, qualitative insights. Consider a balanced approach:

- *Corporate Leaders: Use a combination of quantitative data and qualitative stories from employees and customers.*
- *Small Business Owners: Conduct regular conversations with employees and customers. Combine this with informal feedback to gauge alignment with Servistry principles.*
- *Startup Founders: Track growth indicators like team cohesion, customer feedback, and founder resilience.*
- *Non-Corporate Leaders: Seek feedback from stakeholders through surveys, testimonials, and collaborative reflection.*

In all scenarios, metrics are not merely numbers — they represent stories of service, growth, and leadership.

What Does Success in Servistry Look Like?

The true measure of Servistry isn't confined to performance charts or quarterly reports. Success is visible in thriving employees, loyal customers, resilient communities, and the personal fulfilment of leading with purpose.

As a leader practicing Servistry, ask yourself:

- *Have I created an environment where others can grow and succeed?*
- *Are my decisions reflecting a commitment to serve rather than control?*
- *Have I fostered trust and psychological safety?*
- *How have I grown as a leader by choosing service over authority?*

Ultimately, Servistry is a continuous journey of reflection, growth, and impact. And while metrics provide valuable insights, the most profound indicator is the ripple effect of your service — within your organization and beyond.

CHAPTER TWENTY-ONE

SERVISTRY IN ACTION

Servistry is more than a concept — it's a leadership philosophy that thrives in the real world. When leaders choose to serve their people, customers, and communities, they ignite a chain reaction of trust, loyalty, and growth.

This chapter presents a series of illustrative stories inspired by actual business scenarios. Each narrative highlights how service-led leadership influences decision-making, fosters resilience, and creates lasting value. While the names and details are fictional, the principles remain authentic and universally applicable.

1. A CEO's Choice: People Over Profits

When Liana, the CEO of a mid-sized manufacturing firm, faced a significant financial downturn, her advisors suggested immediate layoffs to protect shareholder value. But Liana, committed to Servistry, chose a different path.

Instead of cutting jobs, she launched a company-wide initiative for cost reduction, inviting employees to contribute ideas. The result was a series of voluntary pay reductions, operational optimizations, and innovative efficiency programs. Transparency was key — Liana held weekly forums to answer questions and offer reassurance.

Outcome: The company not only weathered the crisis but emerged with stronger employee loyalty and operational agility. When the market recovered, Liana's people-first leadership was credited for the turnaround.

2. Empowering the Frontline: The Power of Autonomy

At Lumo Hotels, frontline employees were empowered to resolve guest issues without managerial approval. When a guest's luggage was lost en route, a concierge named Aisha took immediate action. Rather than waiting for corporate protocols, she arranged a same-day shopping experience for essentials, offered complimentary meals, and followed up personally.

Her genuine empathy turned a negative experience into a brand loyalty moment. Because Lumo Hotels valued empowerment and trusted its people, Aisha's decision was celebrated, not questioned.

Outcome: The guest became a lifelong advocate for the brand, sharing their positive experience widely. The hotel's reputation for exceptional service grew organically.

3. Leading with Vulnerability During Crisis

When Mark, a regional director at a logistics company, faced the unexpected loss of a major client, he stood in front of his team — not with polished statements but with genuine vulnerability. He acknowledged the challenge, expressed his own fears, and assured his team that they would navigate it together.

Rather than focusing solely on recovery metrics, Mark asked, "How can I support you in doing your best work during this time?"

Employees responded with innovative ideas to attract new business and reduce costs.

Outcome: Mark's transparent leadership built resilience and inspired trust. The company rebounded within months, with a stronger culture of collaboration.

4. Serving the Community Beyond Business

When a natural disaster struck a region where Nova Tech operated, its leadership didn't just write a donation check. Inspired by Servistry, they mobilized employees to volunteer in relief efforts.

The company provided paid volunteer days, matched employee contributions, and offered resources to support rebuilding initiatives. Leaders personally participated, demonstrating that service wasn't just a corporate value — it was a lived experience.

Outcome: The initiative not only impacted the community but strengthened employee pride and engagement. Nova Tech's commitment to service resonated deeply with both its workforce and customers.

5. Everyday Leadership: Seeing Beyond the Surface

Priya was a mid-level manager who noticed one of her team members, Rahul, had become disengaged and withdrawn. Rather than labelling him as underperforming, she approached him with empathy. Through open dialogue, Priya learned about personal challenges Rahul was facing.

She adjusted his workload temporarily, connected him with resources for support, and continued regular check-ins. Over time, Rahul regained his confidence and excelled in his role.

Outcome: Priya's commitment to serving her team member not only restored Rahul's performance but also built a culture of trust and psychological safety within the team.

Your Servistry Story Awaits

These stories are a reflection of what's possible when leaders embrace Servistry. But the most compelling Servistry story may be the one you create.

- *How will you lead with empathy and purpose?*
- *Where can you empower others to make decisions that serve the greater good?*
- *What ripple effect will your service create in your organization and beyond?*

The true measure of leadership isn't in titles or accolades — it's in the lives you touch and the difference you make.

CHAPTER TWENTY-TWO

SERVISTRY AND THE FUTURE OF WORK

The world of work is shifting at an unprecedented pace. Artificial Intelligence (AI), remote and hybrid work models, and rapidly evolving workplace dynamics are reshaping how we connect, collaborate, and lead. In this evolving environment, the principles of Servistry become not only relevant but essential.

While technology accelerates efficiency and automation, it is the human experience that remains at the heart of leadership. Servistry, with its focus on empathy, purpose, and people-centricity, offers a grounding framework for leaders to navigate uncertainty and thrive in the future of work.

The Rise of AI and Its Ethical Implications

AI is transforming decision-making, automating tasks, and enhancing productivity. Leaders now rely on algorithms to predict trends, assess risks, and personalize customer experiences. However, technology alone cannot account for human values, emotions, or ethical considerations.

A Servistry leader recognizes AI as a tool — not a replacement for human judgment. They ask:

- *Who benefits from this technology?*
- *Are we making decisions that serve our employees, customers, and communities fairly?*
- *How do we mitigate bias and ensure ethical AI practices?*

Instead of fearing AI, Servistry leaders embrace it responsibly, ensuring that technological progress aligns with service-led values. They cultivate a workplace where employees are empowered to work alongside AI, enhancing creativity and innovation rather than replacing human contributions.

Remote and Hybrid Work: Building Connection Without Proximity

The traditional workplace has shifted and so has the concept of presence. Servistry leaders understand that leadership is no longer bound by physical proximity. In remote and hybrid environments, intentional connection becomes the foundation of service-led leadership.

Rather than relying solely on virtual check-ins or monitoring productivity metrics, they prioritize human connection by:

- *Actively listening during virtual conversations, making space for authentic dialogue.*
- *Recognizing the unique challenges faced by remote employees and providing support.*
- *Creating rituals that build a sense of belonging — from informal team chats to celebrating milestones online.*

A Servistry leader knows that psychological safety transcends location. They foster trust by encouraging vulnerability, sharing personal experiences, and making themselves available — not just as managers, but as mentors and supporters.

Evolving Workplaces: A Focus on Flexibility and Well-Being

The future of work is defined by flexibility — in schedules, career paths, and even job roles. Employees seek purpose-driven work and expect their well-being to be prioritized. Servistry leaders respond by cultivating an environment where people feel valued, supported, and empowered to grow.

Consider how a Servistry leader approaches workplace well-being:

- Empathetic Listening: They check in regularly, not just on performance but on personal well-being.
- Flexible Work Models: Understanding that life isn't confined to a 9-to-5, they empower employees to design schedules that balance work and personal priorities.
- Continuous Development: They provide learning opportunities that align with employees' goals and aspirations, supporting both career growth and personal fulfilment.

A Glimpse into the Servistry-Driven Future

Imagine a future where companies measure success not solely by financial metrics but by the well-being of their people and the positive impact they create. Leaders prioritize purpose alongside profit. AI augments human strengths rather than replacing them. Remote teams feel deeply connected, bonded by shared values rather than office walls.

This isn't a distant vision — it's a future that Servistry leaders are actively building today. And as workplaces continue to evolve, the need for leaders who serve will only grow stronger.

Your Role in Shaping the Future

No matter your title or role, you have the power to lead with Servistry. Whether you're managing a global team, collaborating across time zones, or navigating technological advancements, your commitment to serving others defines your leadership.

So, as you look ahead to the future of work, consider this:

- *How can you humanize your leadership in a digital age?*
- *Where can you advocate for fairness, inclusion, and well-being?*
- *How will you use technology to enhance — not diminish — the human experience?*

The future of work is unwritten. But one thing remains certain: Servistry will continue to be a guiding light, illuminating the path forward with purpose, empathy, and unwavering dedication to serving others.

CHAPTER TWENTY-THREE

COACHING AND MENTORING IN SERVISTRY

I often think back to the leaders who shaped my perspective. Some of them coached me with thoughtful questions that unlocked new ways of thinking. Others mentored me, offering reflections from their own journeys. But what made the most profound difference wasn't their authority — it was their service. They weren't just teaching leadership. They were embodying it.

In Servistry, leadership is not a solo endeavour. Its true measure is reflected in how we elevate others. Coaching and mentoring are two of the most powerful tools for spreading this mindset. But unlike traditional approaches, Servistry adds a distinct lens — one that puts the growth of others at the forefront.

When Service Guides the Conversation

Early in my career, I once sought guidance from a leader I deeply admired. I came to her with a problem I believed had only one solution. But instead of providing an answer, she asked:

"How would you approach this if your goal was to serve, not solve?"

That question stayed with me. It shifted my thinking. Suddenly, the problem became an opportunity — not to prove my competence, but to better understand the needs of those around me.

This is the essence of Servistry coaching. It's not about providing answers. It's about awakening perspectives. It's the belief that people already possess much of the insight they seek; they simply need space to access it.

Coaching in Servistry: A Different Kind of Conversation

I recall coaching a mid-level manager who struggled with team morale. She believed her role was to deliver directives and hold people accountable. Yet, through our conversations, she discovered a deeper role — one of support and understanding.

I remember asking her:

"What would it look like to serve your team through this challenge?"

"What might they need from you that they aren't expressing?"

As we spoke, her frustration shifted to curiosity. By the end of our session, she wasn't focused on control but on how she could create an environment where her team felt empowered.

That's the power of Servistry in coaching. It's not transactional; it's transformational. Every question is an invitation to reflect, every silence a moment for clarity.

Mentoring Through the Lens of Servistry

While coaching often focuses on self-discovery, mentoring is the gift of experience. It's a deliberate choice to share the lessons learned — not to prescribe a path, but to illuminate possibilities.

I remember a time when a colleague, just stepping into leadership, asked for my mentorship. She wanted advice on navigating difficult decisions. Instead of simply offering suggestions, I shared a personal story — a moment when I, too, faced uncertainty.

I spoke about the discomfort of making choices without all the answers, and how I had once prioritized short-term results over people. But I also shared what I learned — that the courage to serve, even when the outcomes are uncertain, is what defines a leader.

By the end of our conversation, her anxiety had eased. Not because I had given her a solution, but because she now saw her uncertainty as part of the journey.

In Servistry mentoring, vulnerability is a strength. Our experiences — both our successes and missteps — become valuable tools to guide others.

Creating a Ripple Effect

One of the most rewarding moments in leadership is seeing those you've coached or mentored pay it forward. I've seen mentees become mentors, coaching others with the same spirit of service that once guided them. This ripple effect is the heartbeat of Servistry.

It's why organizations that embrace a service-led culture often experience lasting transformation. Leaders at all levels become enablers of growth. Conversations shift from performance management to potential development. Accountability is no longer feared; it's welcomed — because it comes from a place of care.

A Personal Commitment

As you reflect on your own leadership journey, consider this:

- *Who has been a Servistry leader in your life?*
- *What conversations shaped your growth?*
- *Whom can you now serve through coaching or mentoring?*

True leadership is not defined by how many people report to you, but by how many people grow because of you. Servistry challenges us to leave behind a legacy of empowered leaders — people who, like us, carry forward the commitment to serve.

And when you see the next leader rise, not by standing on your shoulders but because you've helped them find their own footing, you'll know — that is Servistry in its most powerful form.

CHAPTER TWENTY-FOUR

PERSONAL GROWTH THROUGH SERVISTRY

The first time I truly understood Servistry wasn't when I led a team. It wasn't when I managed complex projects or delivered results. It was when I confronted myself — my limitations, my fears, and the question that every leader must eventually face:

Am I willing to grow, not just for myself, but for the people I serve?

Leadership, at its core, is a mirror. Every decision we make, every reaction we have, reflects who we are within. Servistry invites us to stand in front of that mirror without turning away. It challenges us to cultivate self-mastery — not for the sake of power or recognition, but to serve with greater depth and authenticity.

This chapter is not about the external markers of leadership. It's about the internal shifts — the growth that happens when we lead from a place of service.

The Unseen Work of Leadership

There's a misconception that leaders grow primarily through achievements — the promotions, the milestones, the accolades. But the real growth often happens in the spaces no one else sees.

It happens in the pause before responding to a difficult question.

It happens when we choose patience over pride.

It happens when we listen to understand, rather than to reply.

I recall a time when a challenging conversation with a colleague pushed me to my limits. Every instinct urged me to defend my stance, to assert control. But somewhere in that moment, I asked myself:

What would it mean to serve in this conversation, not dominate it?

That single shift — from ego to empathy — transformed not only the conversation but my understanding of leadership itself.

Self-mastery is not the absence of emotion. It is the ability to hold our emotions with awareness and choose how we respond. And every time we do, we strengthen the very muscles that make us Servistry leaders.

Facing the Fear of Vulnerability

One of the most profound lessons in my Servistry journey was understanding that growth requires vulnerability.

As leaders, we often fear being perceived as weak. We hesitate to admit when we don't have the answers. But Servistry teaches us that strength is not in knowing everything — it's in being willing to learn, unlearn, and grow.

I remember the first time I stood in front of my team and admitted a mistake. My voice trembled, but I spoke anyway. What I expected was judgment. What I received was trust.

When we choose transparency over perfection, we create psychological safety — a space where others feel empowered to grow, too.

Vulnerability, when embraced, becomes one of the greatest accelerators of personal growth.

The Discipline of Reflection

Servistry also calls us to the practice of reflection. Not the fleeting kind that happens between meetings, but the intentional pause — the kind that asks:

- *What did I learn today?*
- *Where did I act from fear, and where did I act from service?*
- *How did I contribute to the growth of others?*

I've found that the most impactful leaders are often those who commit to this internal dialogue. They aren't afraid to confront uncomfortable truths. They seek feedback not as validation, but as a mirror for growth.

In fact, the questions that serve us best are often the ones we avoid. And yet, it is in sitting with those questions that we grow beyond the limits we once accepted.

Letting Go to Grow

Perhaps one of the hardest lessons Servistry teaches us is that growth often requires letting go — of outdated beliefs, limiting narratives, and the need for control.

There was a time when I equated leadership with being the one who had all the answers. I held tightly to decisions, fearing that delegation would dilute my influence. But Servistry taught me otherwise.

True leadership is not about holding on. It's about creating the conditions for others to rise.

When I learned to trust my team, not only did they grow — I grew too. My role shifted from problem-solver to enabler. I began to see leadership as a shared responsibility, not a solitary pursuit.

And in that surrender, I found freedom.

A Continuous Journey

Personal growth through Servistry is not a milestone we reach — it's a continuous journey. Every challenge becomes an opportunity for growth. Every relationship becomes a classroom. And every act of service becomes a reflection of the leader we are becoming.

As you walk your own path of self-mastery, I invite you to ask yourself:

- *What part of my leadership journey am I resisting?*
- *Where is growth calling me, even if it feels uncomfortable?*
- *How can I lead in a way that serves not just my goals, but the people around me?*

Because in the end, the most powerful legacy a leader can leave is not just the impact they made — it's the growth they inspired, both in others and within themselves.

That is the essence of Servistry. And that is the path of self-mastery.

Phase – V

Servistry Legacy

CHAPTER TWENTY-FIVE

SERVISTRY BEYOND BUSINESS

I often find myself reflecting on how the principles of Servistry extend far beyond the walls of corporate offices and boardrooms. While business leaders benefit from adopting a service-first mindset, the true power of Servistry is most evident in the everyday choices we make — in our families, communities, and personal relationships.

The essence of Servistry isn't confined to quarterly goals or strategic plans. It's the commitment to serving others with genuine intent, creating ripples of positive impact. To understand how Servistry can shape life itself, I've often asked myself: What if we viewed every interaction as an opportunity to serve?

Leading at Home

One of the most humbling realizations of Servistry is that leadership doesn't require a title. In our homes, we often lead by example — through patience, understanding, and support. I remember a time when a family member faced a particularly difficult decision. My instinct was to offer solutions, but instead, I paused, practiced active listening, and simply asked, "How can I support you?"

That question, devoid of judgment or imposition, opened a space for reflection and clarity. Much like in leadership, sometimes the most profound service is to offer presence rather than direction. Servistry at home is about nurturing emotional safety, celebrating individual growth, and acknowledging that support often means empowering others to find their own way.

Service in Our Communities

The concept of Servistry also shines when we step into our communities. I've seen it in volunteers dedicating time to local causes, mentors guiding young minds, and neighbour's offering small acts of kindness. Each gesture — whether grand or subtle — is a testament to the belief that serving others is a responsibility we all share.

I recall attending a community leadership event where a local leader shared how they transformed a struggling neighbourhood by uniting people through shared purpose. The initiative was not fuelled by external funding or elaborate strategies, but by a simple, powerful question: "What can we do for one another?"

The result was not only revitalized public spaces but also a newfound sense of belonging. Servistry reminds us that leadership is about amplifying collective potential, not seeking individual recognition.

Applying Servistry in Difficult Moments

Perhaps the most profound application of Servistry emerges in challenging situations. Whether it's navigating conflict, supporting a friend in crisis, or simply standing up for what's right, leading with a service mindset requires courage. It's about choosing empathy over judgment, understanding over assumption.

In one of my more difficult conversations, I was faced with differing opinions that seemed irreconcilable. Every part of me wanted to prove my point, but I reminded myself of the principles of Servistry. Rather than react, I listened. I sought to understand the underlying concerns and validate perspectives I hadn't previously considered.

That shift — from proving to understanding — transformed the dialogue. Servistry teaches us that resolution is not about winning; it's about restoring trust and finding pathways forward.

The Ripple Effect of Servistry

The beauty of Servistry is that it multiplies. When we serve without expectation, we inspire others to do the same. I've seen this ripple effect in simple ways — a colleague paying kindness forward, a mentee becoming a mentor, or a family member choosing patience over frustration.

It's a reminder that leadership, at its core, is not a role we step into for designated moments. It's who we are — in how we listen, respond, and contribute. Servistry is a lifelong practice, one that shapes not only the lives of others but also our own character.

As you reflect on your own journey, I invite you to consider where Servistry already exists in your life.

- *Where have you led by serving?*
- *Who has served you in moments of growth or challenge?*
- *How might a service-first mindset change your relationships and impact?*

The world does not merely need more leaders. It needs more Servistry — in homes, neighbourhoods, schools, and communities. It's in the daily choices to offer kindness, lend support, and stand for others. That is the legacy of Servistry — one that extends far beyond business, leaving an enduring mark on the world.

And it starts with us.

CHAPTER TWENTY-SIX

THE GENERATIONAL IMPACT OF SERVISTRY

Leadership is often measured by immediate results — the successful projects, the market gains, the celebrated milestones. But the true measure of a leader is far greater. It's found in the ripples they create — the lessons they impart, the values they uphold, and the people they influence. Servistry, when embraced with conviction, does not end with one leader's journey. It extends beyond, shaping generations to come.

I've often reflected on the people who influenced my leadership — mentors, family members, even colleagues who unknowingly taught me what it means to lead with service. What stands out is not their achievements, but how they made others feel. Their legacy was not built on titles or accolades, but on the courage to uplift others, to listen deeply, and to create space for growth.

But how do we ensure that Servistry lives on? How do we plant seeds of service-led leadership that continue to flourish, even when we step away?

The Unseen Influence

Legacy is rarely a single grand gesture. It's found in the seemingly small choices — the conversation that sparked confidence in a hesitant voice, the moment of support that shifted someone's belief in their potential, the encouragement that ignited resilience.

I recall a leader I worked with early in my career. They weren't the loudest in the room, nor the most decorated. But they had an unmatched presence — a willingness to listen, a humility that invited others to speak, and a dedication to amplifying the strengths of those around them. I wasn't just learning business acumen from them; I was witnessing Servistry in action.

Years later, I found myself repeating their words of encouragement to someone facing similar doubts. It dawned on me then — legacies aren't simply remembered; they are relived. Each act of Servistry has the power to echo through others.

Shaping the Next Generation

When we lead through Servistry, we nurture the kind of leadership that transcends individual success. And it starts with a question we must ask ourselves: What values am I passing on?

In organizations, this means creating cultures where service-led leadership is not an exception but the norm. It means mentoring not for compliance, but for growth — encouraging others to lead with empathy, curiosity, and integrity. Every conversation, every decision becomes an opportunity to model Servistry.

Beyond workplaces, Servistry extends to the lessons we teach our children, the values we share with our communities, and the examples we set in times of uncertainty. Imagine a generation raised not solely on competition and ambition, but on the belief that leadership is about service. That belief, when nurtured, can transform families, schools, and societies.

Legacy Through Actions, Not Words

One of the most profound truths about Servistry is that it is rarely spoken; it is shown. Those who experience its impact are often the ones who carry it forward, without prompting. The gratitude of being led with empathy becomes the foundation of how they lead others.

In moments of challenge, I've seen individuals recall the influence of a service-first leader and choose to act with similar compassion. It's a cycle that perpetuates itself — not out of obligation, but because Servistry leaves a lasting imprint.

And isn't that the kind of legacy we wish to create? Not one bound to personal recognition, but one that empowers others to lead in their own right.

Building Your Leadership Legacy

Legacy is not something we write at the end of our careers. It's something we write every day, in the way we show up. Consider these reflections as you think about your own Servistry legacy:

- *Who are the people who shaped your understanding of service-led leadership?*
- *What lessons from their leadership have stayed with you?*
- *How can you intentionally pass those lessons forward?*

Your legacy will not be determined by the number of people who remember your name, but by the number of people who remember how you made them feel — empowered, seen, and valued.

That is the generational impact of Servistry. It's the belief that leadership is not confined to a moment in time. It lives on in the choices we inspire others to make.

And those choices, in turn, continue the story — a story of service, growth, and enduring leadership.

And as you walk this path of Servistry, know that your legacy is already in motion.

CHAPTER TWENTY-SEVEN

FROM SERVISTRY TO MOVEMENT

Movements aren't born from grand declarations. They begin in quiet moments — in the spaces where ideas take root, where stories are shared, and where people discover a collective belief in something greater than themselves. Servistry, when practiced with sincerity, has the potential to transcend the walls of businesses and organizations. It becomes a philosophy that ripples through communities, igniting a movement of service-led leadership.

But how does a philosophy become a movement? And what role do we, as individuals, play in that transformation?

The First Ripple

I remember the first time I saw Servistry move beyond the workplace. It wasn't through a formal initiative or a leadership mandate. It was a leader who, in their quiet way, carried their belief in service into their neighbourhoods. They mentored young people, volunteered their time, and brought the same care and listening they offered their colleagues to those in their community. There was no announcement of their efforts — no expectation of recognition. It was simply who they were.

And soon, others followed. Not because they were asked, but because they were inspired. Servistry had become a way of being, and that authenticity invited others to embody the same.

This is how movements are born — not through force, but through example. Every act of service plants a seed, and when those seeds are nurtured, they grow into something far greater than one person's efforts.

Servistry in Action — Beyond Business

Communities are where the truest forms of Servistry are often revealed. Unlike structured corporate settings, the needs in communities are diverse and deeply human. And yet, the principles remain the same:

- **Empathy as a Guide**: Understanding the lived experiences of others is the foundation of meaningful service. Listening without assumption and leading without agenda cultivates trust.
- **Empowerment Over Control**: In thriving communities, leaders are not those who seek authority, but those who create space for others to rise. Servistry encourages shared leadership.
- **Sustainability Through Service**: True service isn't a one-time act. It's a commitment to long-term impact — building systems that uplift, educate, and sustain growth.

I've seen Servistry emerge in unexpected places — in community kitchens where volunteers lead with dignity, in mentorship programs where young people find guidance, and in grassroots movements where neighbours come together to solve challenges. What unites them is a belief that leadership is not a title, but a responsibility to serve.

From Leader to Catalyst

When we shift from practicing Servistry to catalysing it, our leadership takes on new meaning. Instead of simply offering our service, we begin to inspire others to do the same. We become stewards of a movement — amplifying the voices of those around us and empowering them to lead.

This is not the kind of leadership that seeks visibility. It is the kind that finds fulfilment in watching others step forward. Servistry is not possessive. It grows strongest when it is shared.

And the most remarkable part? You may never fully see the extent of your impact. A word of encouragement, a gesture of kindness, or a decision made with empathy — these moments often carry on, influencing others in ways we'll never know.

Your Role in the Movement

The question now is not whether Servistry can become a movement. It already is. Every individual who chooses to lead through service contributes to its momentum. The real question is: How will you participate?

- **Look Beyond Your Circle**: Servistry is not confined to the workplace. It thrives in families, neighbourhoods, schools, and social initiatives. Where can your leadership serve others?
- **Pass It Forward:** Mentorship is one of the most powerful ways to sustain the philosophy of Servistry. Who in your life could benefit from your guidance and encouragement?
- **Share the Stories:** Stories fuel movements. By sharing your experiences of service-led leadership, you invite others to reflect on their own impact.

A Movement Without an End

Servistry is not meant to be contained. It's a mindset that, once embraced, naturally finds its way into every facet of life. It is leadership that exists not for personal gain, but for collective good. And because it is rooted in service, its influence is limitless.

Long after we've stepped away from our formal roles, the essence of Servistry will remain — in the lives we've touched, the leaders we've nurtured, and the communities we've strengthened. That is the true mark of a movement.

And so, as you continue your journey, know this: Every act of Servistry, no matter how small, adds to a story far greater than your own. A story of leaders who serve, communities that rise, and a movement that endures.

CHAPTER TWENTY-EIGHT

COMMON PITFALLS & CHALLENGES

Servistry — the intentional practice of leading through service — is a powerful and transformative leadership approach. Yet, for all its merits, not every leader readily adopts it. Why? The reasons are often layered, influenced by personal mindsets, organizational cultures, and external pressures.

Having navigated both the triumphs and challenges of Servistry, I've seen firsthand what holds leaders back. Understanding these obstacles isn't about criticism — it's about clarity. When we name the challenges, we empower ourselves to confront them.

The Fear of Perceived Weakness

One of the most pervasive misconceptions about Servistry is that serving others diminishes authority. Some leaders believe that to serve is to submit, risking their credibility or power. This belief is especially prevalent in environments that celebrate dominance over collaboration.

I once worked alongside a leader who was hesitant to show vulnerability. They equated "service" with "softness" and feared that leading with empathy would compromise their strength. But what they didn't initially realize was that service, when rooted in clarity and conviction, commands respect. It strengthens trust and deepens influence — not by force, but by earned loyalty.

The Truth: Servistry does not undermine authority. It amplifies it through trust, integrity, and genuine connection.

The Ego Barrier

Leadership often comes with praise and recognition. And while it's natural to take pride in accomplishments, unchecked ego can obstruct Servistry. Leaders driven by a need for validation may hesitate to empower others or share credit. The mindset of "I must be the one in control" can stifle collaboration and diminish the contributions of others.

I recall a moment when I personally struggled with this. Early in my career, I believed that being the 'solution provider' was the mark of a strong leader. It took time — and moments of hard reflection — to understand that true leadership isn't measured by how much I personally achieve, but by how effectively I elevate those around me.

The Truth: Servistry requires humility. The greatest leaders are those who lead without needing to be the loudest voice in the room.

Short-Term Pressure vs. Long-Term Impact

In organizations where immediate results are prized above all else, leaders often feel pressured to prioritize short-term gains. Servistry, with its emphasis on people-centric leadership, may seem like a slower path to success. After all, investing in people, building trust, and fostering collaboration takes time.

But what I've learned — and what countless organizations have demonstrated — is that Servistry doesn't delay results; it sustains them. When leaders serve their teams, they create environments of psychological safety, innovation, and accountability. These are the very factors that drive long-term growth.

The Truth: Servistry is not a trade-off. It's an investment that compounds over time, resulting in both people growth and business success.

Lack of Self-Awareness

Some leaders unknowingly resist Servistry simply because they haven't yet reflected on their leadership style. Without intentional self-assessment, it's easy to assume one is leading effectively without recognizing the subtle gaps in how they engage with others.

I've facilitated leadership workshops where accomplished executives came face-to-face with the realization that their well-intentioned behaviours were unintentionally disengaging their teams. Moments like these are not failures — they are opportunities. The willingness to reflect and grow is itself an act of Servistry.

The Truth: Servistry begins with self-awareness. Leaders who embrace honest introspection can break free from ineffective patterns and lead with greater purpose.

The Misalignment of Organizational Culture

Even the most committed Servistry leaders can face resistance in environments that value individual achievement over collective success. In organizations with toxic competition, distrust, or poor communication, the principles of Servistry may feel at odds with the prevailing culture.

But leadership, even in challenging environments, is contagious.

I've seen leaders act as catalysts for change simply by modelling Servistry — creating ripples that gradually shift cultural norms. It's not easy, and it requires courage, but every act of service stands as a quiet rebellion against toxic leadership.

The Truth: Servistry can thrive even in difficult environments. Every leader who embodies it becomes a force for cultural transformation.

Overcoming the Pitfalls

So, how do we navigate these challenges? It starts with intentionality:

- *Recognize the fear. If the idea of Servistry feels uncomfortable, ask yourself why. Is it fear of perception? Fear of failure? Naming the fear lessens its power.*
- *Commit to humility. Embrace feedback and view it not as criticism but as a pathway to growth.*
- *Challenge short-term thinking. Prioritize sustainable impact over temporary gains.*
- *Cultivate self-awareness. Reflect regularly, seek mentorship, and listen to the voices of those you lead.*
- *Be the culture you wish to see. Even if your organization resists Servistry, lead as though it doesn't. Your leadership can inspire change.*

The Courage to Serve

Every leader faces moments of doubt. Servistry isn't about perfection — it's about persistence. The most impactful leaders I've known were not those who never stumbled, but those who stood up again, choosing to serve even when it was difficult.

As you continue your journey, remember this: The barriers to Servistry are not immovable. They are invitations — to grow, to reflect, and to lead with greater purpose. And in overcoming them, you not only transform your own leadership — you become a beacon for others to do the same.

Servistry is not the absence of challenge. It is the choice to lead through it.

CHAPTER TWENTY-NINE

THE SERVISTRY COMMITMENT

Servistry is not a one-time act. It's not a concept to reflect on during leadership workshops and then set aside when the real work begins. Servistry, at its core, is a way of being — a choice leaders make, day in and day out, to serve their teams, organizations, and communities.

But how does one translate the principles of Servistry into a consistent, lived experience? In my journey, I've learned that the most significant shifts happen not through grand gestures but through intentional daily actions. Servistry is built in the quiet moments — in the questions we ask, the attention we give, and the courage we show.

This chapter is an invitation to reflect, act, and commit. A call to turn Servistry from an aspiration into a defining leadership practice.

Why Commitment Matters

Leadership is filled with competing priorities. Metrics demand attention. Deadlines loom. And in the rush of the day, it's easy to push service to the margins.

But the leaders I admire most are those who remain steadfast in their commitment to Servistry, even when it's inconvenient. They choose empathy when frustration would be easier. They listen when they could dictate. They uplift others without fearing that it diminishes their own standing.

I've faced these choices myself. And I've come to understand that the moments where Servistry feels the hardest — when time is scarce, emotions are high, or uncertainty prevails — are the very moments where it matters most.

The Three Anchors of Daily Servistry

To make Servistry a daily habit, I've found it helpful to anchor leadership around three simple, powerful commitments:

1. Commit to Awareness

Every interaction is an opportunity to lead with service. But we can't serve effectively if we're unaware — unaware of our impact, the needs of others, or the dynamics at play.

- Start your day with intention. Ask, "Who can I serve today, and how?"
- Practice active listening. Give people your full attention. Resist the urge to respond quickly — seek to understand first.
- Notice the unnoticed. Is there someone whose contributions often go unseen? A challenge that remains unspoken? Servistry requires presence — noticing beyond what's obvious.

2. Commit to Courageous Action

- Service-led leadership often calls for courage. Courage to stand up for others, to challenge the status quo, or to take responsibility when mistakes occur. It's a choice to act, even when silence would be safer.
-
- Use your voice for good. Speak up for fairness and inclusion. Servistry isn't passive — it's active advocacy.
- Empower others. Delegate not just tasks, but trust. Invite others to step into leadership and celebrate their growth.
- Admit when you're wrong. Vulnerability builds trust. Servistry leaders own their mistakes and learn from them.

3. Commit to Reflection

Servistry thrives in leaders who reflect — who pause to consider their actions, their motives, and their growth. Reflection keeps us aligned with our values and ensures we remain intentional in our leadership.

- End your day with reflection. Ask, "Did I lead with service today? Where could I have done better?"
- Welcome feedback. Invite honest perspectives from your team. Servistry leaders are lifelong learners.
- Practice gratitude. Reflect on the people you had the opportunity to serve, and recognize how they, in turn, contributed to your growth.

The Power of Micro-Moments

While leadership books often celebrate monumental decisions,

Servistry is often practiced in micro-moments — those small, fleeting opportunities where we choose to lead with empathy, humility, and intention.

- Taking an extra minute to check in on a colleague's well-being. • Offering words of appreciation without waiting for a milestone.
- Pausing to listen when a disagreement arises, rather than rushing to defend your point.
- Recognizing the invisible efforts of those who work behind the scenes.

These moments may seem insignificant, but they build cultures of trust and belonging. And over time, they define the kind of leader you are.

Your Personal Servistry Commitment

As we near the conclusion of this book, I invite you to reflect on your personal Servistry commitment. What will it look like in your leadership practice?

Consider these questions:

- *What does Servistry mean to you?*
- *Who has exemplified Servistry in your life? How did they impact you?*
- *What is one Servistry principle you can commit to practicing daily?*
- *How will you hold yourself accountable for leading with service?*

There is no perfect answer. Servistry is not about flawless leadership — it's about intentional, human leadership. It's about choosing to lead in service of others, knowing that in doing so, we become the best versions of ourselves.

A Continuous Journey

Servistry isn't a destination. It's not a title to achieve or a certificate to hang on the wall. It's a practice — one that grows with you, evolves through your experiences, and deepens with every act of service.

And the beauty of it? Every single day presents a new opportunity to choose Servistry.

As you step forward from this chapter, remember that the commitment you make to Servistry isn't just for your teams or your organization. It's for yourself. Because to lead with service is to lead with purpose — and there's no leadership journey more rewarding than that.

The Servistry commitment begins now. And it begins with you.

CHAPTER THIRTY

EMPHASISING SERVISTRY AS A MOVEMENT

The world doesn't change because of a single decision. It changes when that decision inspires others to act, creating ripples far beyond what one person could achieve alone. Servistry, at its core, is not just a leadership approach — it is a call to action. What begins as an individual commitment to serve can grow into a collective movement, redefining how we lead, collaborate, and succeed.

From Individual Practice to Collective Impact

I remember the moment I first understood that Servistry wasn't just about my own leadership. It was during a conversation with a colleague who had embraced the principles of serving others without expecting immediate rewards. They shared how their small but intentional acts of service had sparked curiosity in their team. What started as a leadership choice became a cultural shift. People began to support one another, not because they were asked to, but because it felt right.

This is how movements begin. Servistry grows not through

mandates or programs but through stories — stories of leaders who chose empathy over authority, integrity over shortcuts, and collective growth over personal gain.

The Courage to Go First

Embracing Servistry requires courage. In a world often fixated on results and competition, leading with service can feel like swimming against the tide. But as we've explored throughout this book, the most impactful leaders are those who dare to lead differently. When you embody Servistry, you show others what's possible. You model a kind of leadership that values people as much as performance.

And courage is contagious. When people witness the power of Servistry in action, they are more likely to adopt it themselves. The small choices — listening with intent, empowering others, celebrating contributions — create visible change. Over time, these choices become a shared belief system, turning Servistry into a cultural norm.

Scaling Servistry Beyond Organizations

While Servistry often begins within an organization, its influence rarely stops there. Imagine a leader who fosters psychological safety within their team, encouraging open dialogue and respectful disagreement. That same leader, when volunteering in their community or mentoring young professionals, will naturally apply those same principles. Servistry transcends titles and industries. It is equally valuable in nonprofit work, education, entrepreneurship, and even family dynamics.

The true power of Servistry is unlocked when it becomes a mindset that shapes how we engage with the world. Consider how organizations with a strong service culture often inspire their customers and partners. Businesses that treat their employees with care are more likely to see those employees become brand ambassadors. Servistry, when embraced collectively, builds ecosystems of trust and collaboration.

Your Role in the Servistry Movement

Movements are not built by leaders at the top. They are built by individuals who choose to embody a philosophy and share it with others. You may already be doing this — in the way you mentor a colleague, advocate for inclusive decision-making, or take the time to recognize the efforts of your team. Each act of Servistry, no matter how small, has the potential to inspire others.

But intentionality matters. As you continue your leadership journey, consider how you can amplify the movement:

- **Tell your story**: Share moments when Servistry has made a difference in your leadership or in the lives of those around you.
- **Recognize and celebrate**: Encourage others who demonstrate Servistry. Acknowledgement fuels commitment.
- **Mentor with purpose**: Use your experiences to guide others in adopting a service-first mindset.
- **Advocate for systemic change**: Support policies and structures that prioritize people-centric leadership in your organization.

Servistry becomes a movement when leaders choose to lead not just for personal success, but for the collective good.

A Future Shaped by Servistry

As we look ahead, the need for Servistry has never been greater. Technological disruption, economic uncertainty, and shifting workplace expectations demand leaders who are adaptable, empathetic, and purpose-driven. Servistry provides the foundation for navigating these challenges with integrity.

But beyond the workplace, Servistry offers a vision for how we can build better communities and a more inclusive society. When service-led leadership becomes the norm, collaboration replaces competition, trust replaces fear, and progress is measured not just in financial terms, but in human impact.

You are now part of this movement. The question is no longer whether Servistry works — it is how far you are willing to take it.

In the next chapter, we will distil the essential principles of Servistry, ensuring that this movement has a clear and actionable foundation. Let's explore what it means to carry the spirit of Servistry forward, not just as leaders, but as catalysts for lasting change.

PRINCIPLES OF SERVISTRY

The strength of any leadership philosophy lies in its clarity and adaptability. Servistry is no exception. While its essence is rooted in the belief that leadership is a service to others, translating that belief into everyday actions requires a strong foundation of principles. These principles serve as both a compass and a commitment — guiding leaders through complexity while ensuring they remain grounded in purpose.

As I reflect on my own leadership journey, I can trace countless moments where these principles came to life. They weren't always perfect, nor were they without challenges. But every decision I made with Servistry in mind brought greater clarity, deeper connection, and more enduring success. These principles are not theoretical ideals; they are practical, actionable truths that shape how we lead, collaborate, and grow.

1. Service Before Self

At the heart of Servistry is the belief that true leadership is about putting others first. This doesn't mean neglecting your own well-being or ambitions. Instead, it means recognizing that the success of your team, your organization, and your community is the ultimate reflection of your leadership.

I've seen leaders who relentlessly pursued personal accolades, only to find their influence fleeting. In contrast, leaders who prioritized service-built teams that thrived, cultures that endured, and legacies that inspired. Serving others is not a sign of weakness; it is the greatest demonstration of strength.

Ask yourself:

- *Am I making decisions that prioritize the growth and well-being of others?*
- *Do my actions reflect a commitment to collective success over personal gain?*

2. Empathy as a Leadership Strength

Empathy is not just a soft skill — it is a leadership superpower. Understanding the perspectives, challenges, and aspirations of those around you enables better decision-making and stronger relationships. Servistry calls on leaders to listen without judgment, act with compassion, and create spaces where people feel seen and valued.

Some of my most humbling leadership moments were those when I chose to listen, even when I disagreed. By setting aside assumptions and truly seeking to understand, I not only resolved conflicts but also built lasting trust.

Ask yourself:

- *How often do I listen with the intent to understand, rather than to respond?*
- *Am I creating a culture where empathy is valued and practiced?*

3. Leading with Integrity

Integrity in Servistry means leading with honesty, transparency, and consistency. It is the quiet, unwavering commitment to doing what is right, even when no one is watching. Integrity fosters trust — and without trust, leadership cannot exist.

There were moments when making the right decision meant facing discomfort or challenge. But every time I chose integrity over convenience, the respect and loyalty I earned far outweighed the temporary difficulty. Leaders who embody Servistry hold themselves accountable to the highest standards, knowing their influence shapes not only results but also the moral fabric of their organizations.

Ask yourself:

- *Do my actions align with my values, even when faced with adversity?*
- *How can I build a culture where integrity is not only expected but celebrated?*

4. Growth Through Service

In Servistry, leadership is not a static state. It is a continuous journey of learning and growth. By embracing curiosity, seeking feedback, and remaining open to change, leaders expand their capacity to serve. Growth through service means viewing every challenge as an opportunity to deepen understanding and refine leadership.

I've often found that the most significant lessons came from moments of struggle — when a project failed, a decision backfired, or a team member voiced dissatisfaction. Servistry taught me not to retreat from these moments but to lean into them. Every setback offered a chance to grow stronger and serve better.

Ask yourself:

- *Am I actively seeking opportunities to learn and grow through my leadership experiences?*
- *Do I encourage growth in others by providing support, feedback, and opportunities for development?*

5. Creating a Ripple Effect

The true measure of Servistry is not the leader's success but the success of those they serve. Servistry leaders create a ripple effect — empowering others to lead, fostering cultures of service, and inspiring movements that extend far beyond their immediate influence.

I think of the leaders who mentored me, those who saw potential I hadn't yet recognized in myself. They didn't just teach me leadership; they instilled in me the responsibility to pass it on. This ripple effect is why Servistry has the power to transform not just organizations, but industries, communities, and societies.

Ask yourself:

- *Am I intentionally empowering others to lead?*
- *How can I ensure my influence creates a lasting positive impact?*

Living the Principles of Servistry

These five principles are not separate, nor are they sequential. They are interconnected, each reinforcing and amplifying the others. To live the principles of Servistry is to lead with intentionality — choosing service over status, empathy over ego, and integrity over expediency.

But living these principles also requires grace — both for yourself and for those you lead. You will stumble. You will face moments of doubt. And you will make mistakes. Servistry is not about perfection; it is about the unwavering commitment to grow, learn, and serve despite those challenges.

As you continue your leadership journey, I invite you to return to these principles often. Reflect on how they show up in your decisions, your relationships, and your legacy. Let them guide you through uncertainty and remind you of the profound privilege it is to lead.

In the next and final chapter, we'll explore how these principles come together in The Servistry Way — a lasting commitment to service-led leadership that goes beyond philosophy and becomes a way of life.

CHAPTER THIRTY-TWO

THE SERVISTRY WAY

Servistry is more than a leadership philosophy; it's a way of being. It doesn't live within the confines of corporate strategy or leadership jargon. It breathes in the choices we make daily — how we lead, how we listen, and how we serve. As I write this, I think about the countless moments that shaped my understanding of service-led leadership. Moments when I stumbled, when I hesitated, when I chose comfort over courage. And moments when I didn't.

The Servistry Way isn't about a perfect leader who never falters. It's about the leader who chooses to serve, even when it's hard. Especially when it's hard.

I recall a time when I faced a decision that could have brought a quick win for my organization but would have compromised the well-being of the people involved. The pressure to deliver results was immense. Logic and timelines battled against the voice within — the one that asked, "But at what cost?" In that moment, I understood what it meant to lead through Servistry. Not in theory, but in practice. I chose the harder path. The longer one. Because leading with service is not a convenient choice; it's a conscious one.

That's the Servistry Way.

Living the Servistry Way

But how does one truly live it? I've often pondered this. You don't wake up one day and declare yourself a Servistry leader. There's no grand announcement. It starts in the smallest of decisions — the willingness to listen when you'd rather speak, to uplift when you'd rather compete, to pause when urgency demands haste.

There's no checklist, no fixed playbook. Yet, there are truths I've held close that have guided me through uncertainty.

First, Servistry begins with presence. In a world of constant noise, leaders are often celebrated for their ability to act swiftly. But some of the most profound leadership I've witnessed came from those who knew when not to act — when to listen instead. There's strength in stillness, and Servistry thrives in those spaces.

Second, it's about resilience. Not the kind that glorifies burnout, but the resilience that comes from knowing why you lead in the first place. Purpose anchors us. It reminds us that leadership is not about how much we control, but how much we contribute. When we lose sight of that, Servistry brings us back.

And third, Servistry demands courage. Not the absence of fear, but the willingness to lead through it. Speaking up for what is right. Defending the voices that go unheard. Making decisions that may not yield immediate applause but serve a greater good. This is where Servistry separates itself from traditional leadership. It refuses to measure success solely by results; it asks, Who did you serve along the way?

The Legacy You Leave

When I think of legacy, I no longer think of titles or accolades. I think of faces. Conversations. Moments of trust built over time. Leaders may not remember every strategic decision you made, but they will remember how you made them feel. Did they feel valued? Empowered? Seen?

The Servistry Way ensures that they do.

It's not bound by industry or geography. It's just as relevant to a small business owner mentoring their first employee as it is to a global CEO navigating complex decisions. It shapes boardrooms and communities alike. That's the beauty of it — Servistry belongs to anyone willing to lead through service.

And now, it belongs to you.

Your Servistry Commitment

As we close this book, I invite you to make a commitment — not to me, not to the concept of Servistry, but to yourself and those you lead. Commit to leading with purpose, serving others with empathy, and making decisions with integrity.

The Servistry Way does not ask for perfection. It asks for presence. Every day, in every interaction, you have the opportunity to choose service over status, connection over control, and impact over recognition. These choices, repeated consistently, will define your leadership legacy.

While this chapter marks the conclusion of our written journey together, it is only the beginning of yours. Servistry is not static — it grows, evolves, and expands with every leader who chooses to embrace it. As you apply these principles in your own life, you become part of a larger movement — one that has the power to transform organizations, communities, and even the world.

And so, I leave you with one final question:

How will you lead through Servistry?

Let your answer guide you. Let your service define you.

This is the Servistry Way.

P.S.

Dear Readers,

Thank you for taking this journey with me.

Writing Servistry has been more than a pursuit of ideas; it has been a reflection of my own experiences and beliefs. Every story shared, every concept explored, and every insight offered has stemmed from the realization that leadership is most impactful when it is rooted in service.

The path to Servistry is not always straightforward. There were moments in my own leadership when authority felt easier than empathy, and results seemed more tangible than relationships. But time has shown me that the greatest successes come when we prioritize people — when we lead not from a pedestal, but from a place of genuine care and commitment.

This book is not a prescription. It is an invitation. An invitation to lead with courage, to listen deeply, and to serve without the expectation of reward. I believe that every act of service, no matter how small, has the power to ripple outward — influencing teams, communities, and even entire industries.

If Servistry has sparked even a single thought, a question, or a shift in your perspective, then this effort has been worthwhile.

As you return to your organizations, homes, and communities, I encourage you to carry forward the spirit of Servistry. Choose connection over control, purpose over power, and service over self-interest.

The future of leadership is not defined by titles or authority. It is shaped by those who have the courage to serve.

Thank you once again for being part of this movement.

With gratitude and belief in your leadership.

Deepak Sharma
Author of Servistry